Elvis & Olive

ALSO BY STEPHANIE WATSON

Elvis & Olive: Super Detectives

STEPHANIE WATSON

SCHOLASTIC INC.
New York Toronto London Auckland
Sydney Mexico City New Delhi Hong Kong

No part of this publication may be reproduced, stored in a retrieval
system, or transmitted in any form or by any means, electronic,
mechanical, photocopying, recording, or otherwise, without written
permission of the publisher. For information regarding permission,
write to Scholastic Inc., Attention: Permissions Department,
557 Broadway, New York, NY 10012.

This book was originally published in hardcover by
Scholastic Press in 2008.

ISBN 978-0-545-03184-4

12 11 10 9 8 7 6 5 4 3 2 1   10 11 12/0

Printed in the U.S.A.   40
First Scholastic paperback printing, June 2010

Book design by Elizabeth B. Parisi

For Marcelo

I love you, and that's no secret.

Chapter One

The first day of summer vacation stretched in front of Natalie Wallis like a long road with no street signs. It was only ten in the morning and already she missed school. Already, she longed for homework and teachers and tests. Already, summer was boring. So she gave herself an assignment.

See how fast you can ride your bike around the block. Natalie wrote this in extra-neat cursive in a notebook left over from school. She set the notebook in her straw bike basket and zeroed out the stopwatch hanging from her neck. Then she strapped on her helmet and mounted her pink bicycle.

Over and over she rode around the block, passing the same anthills and dried worms and blackened gum dots on the sidewalk. Each time she circled, Natalie refined her course a little more. She learned to avoid the familiar cracks and pits in the concrete. She stopped waving hello to the neighbors as she passed their yards, giving them quick, aerodynamic nods instead. After half an hour, her record was two minutes and twenty seconds.

Not good enough, Natalie thought. *I can beat that.*

She took off again. Her long brown braids swung with each pedal push, her glasses fogged with sweat, and the sidewalk became a gray blur beneath her. The route was so familiar by now, she was able to round each corner at the perfect angle and speed. Natalie turned the last corner and came to the homestretch, the steep hill that led up to her house. *Just a little way to go*, she coached herself.

She resisted the urge to check her time. That would only slow her down. Out of the corner of her eye, she saw her neighbor's white fence. *Just a few more seconds.* To forget the growing burn in her legs, she recalled the plot from the last book she read. *Once there was a young farmer boy who took care of baby wolves and —*

"Hey you! Stop!"

Natalie looked up. Not ten feet ahead, a small, skinny boy stood with his palm shoved out like a traffic cop. She screeched on her brakes to avoid hitting him, her front wheel wobbling to a stop dangerously close to the boy's knees. He didn't flinch.

Natalie forgot all about checking her time on the stopwatch. She forgot about the plot of the wolf book. She forgot everything but this boy who had appeared out of nowhere. She flicked her kickstand down.

"I almost hit you," Natalie said, catching her breath. "You should watch out."

She recognized the boy. He and his dad had moved into the gray house kitty-corner from hers about a month ago. As Natalie left for her private-school bus stop, she would watch him stomp to the public-school bus stop at the other end of the block, whacking his backpack on the fence posts as he went. Some of the kids at Natalie's stop would laugh at him. "What a freak," they'd say. Once the boy got to the corner, he'd throw pebbles at the stop sign. Natalie would listen to the distant metallic pings until his bus came, or hers did.

The boy wasn't wearing a shirt today. From up close, Natalie noticed that his skin was so pale you could see the blue veins underneath, and his chest was covered with scabby mosquito bites. His short, spiky hair was so blond it was almost white.

"You could've gotten hurt," Natalie insisted. "I almost hit you."

He was still holding his hand out, willing Natalie to stay where she was. The other hand was behind his back.

"I'm gonna tell you a secret," he said.

"Why would you tell me a secret?" Natalie asked. "I don't even know you."

"So?"

"Usually you know someone before you tell them a secret," she said, offering her hand to shake his. "I'm Natalie. You're the new boy from across the street, right?"

His eyes became slits.

"Boy?! I'm not a *boy*. I'm a GIRL!" The shout echoed off the houses. Natalie slowly lowered her hand back to the handlebar.

"Oh. Sorry," she said, wincing. "Then why aren't you wearing a shirt?"

"It's *summer*," the girl said, raising one eyebrow. "And it's *hot*."

"Oh," Natalie said again. True, it was hot. But would Natalie ever walk around without a shirt? No. Never. Not even if it was so hot, the grass melted. Not even if the hose water came out boiling.

"Anyway," the girl rolled her eyes, "my name's Annie Beckett. You'll notice that's a *girl's* name."

Natalie scanned Annie's face for clues of her age. Her teeth were coming in large and crooked, like Natalie's. But she still had some baby fat in her cheeks.

She's maybe a year younger than me, Natalie guessed. *Yeah, probably nine.*

"What grade are you in?" Natalie asked.

Annie groaned. "I'm not in a grade," she said. "It's *summer.* Do you want to know my secret or not?"

"Okay, okay," Natalie said.

"If I tell you," Annie said, dropping her voice to a whisper, "you can't tell anyone."

"I won't."

Annie came to the side of the bike and cupped a sweaty hand to Natalie's ear. Her breath smelled like cheese puffs.

"I found a baby bird," she whispered. "I have it right here."

"Really?" Natalie said. "Let me see."

Annie brought her other hand from behind her back, her fingers closed in a careful fist. Her fingernails were bitten down to nubs and outlined in black grime. She slowly opened her hand to reveal a tiny, pale bird. It had a bald, pink head and dark blue eyeballs that showed through its transparent eyelids. After a few seconds, the bird hadn't moved. Natalie touched one of the naked wings with a nervous finger.

"Is it okay?" she asked.

Annie stifled a giggle. "It's dead."

"Ew!" Natalie cried, jerking her finger away. "You're sick." She gripped her handlebars and snapped up the kickstand.

"Wait!" Annie said, shoving the bird roughly into her shorts pocket. "I have another secret for you."

"What, a dog that got hit by a car? No thanks." Natalie rolled her wheel onto the boulevard and pedaled over the thick grass. Before she could ride off, Annie snatched the spiral notebook from the bike basket.

"Hey!" Natalie screeched. "Give that back!" She made a wild grab for the notebook and almost fell off her bike. Annie backed away. She began flipping through the pages.

"Wow, you have nice handwriting," she said.

"Give it back *right now*," Natalie demanded. She

dropped her bike on the grass and charged, but Annie darted out of her grasp.

"I'll give it back if you come see a secret under my porch," Annie said.

"No way." Natalie grabbed at the notebook again, and Annie whisked it out of reach. Despite being so skinny and frail-looking, she was quick.

"Come," Annie said.

"No."

"Then say good-bye to your book," Annie said, skipping off the curb. She paused in the middle of the street to do a little waltz with the notebook, the front and back covers held out like arms of a dance partner. As she whirled onto the opposite boulevard, she shot Natalie a toothy grin.

Natalie sighed and dropped her chin to her chest, knowing she'd have to follow. As she looked down, she saw that the stopwatch around her neck was still counting. She pressed the stop button. Five minutes, forty seconds. For turning a calm summer day completely upside down, it was a new record.

Chapter Two

Natalie jogged to catch up with Annie, who was now dancing across her weedy front lawn, beheading white dandelion puffs with each step. When Natalie got close enough, she again tried to snatch the notebook, but it was no use. Annie simply yanked it away and kept waltzing to her imaginary tune.

When Annie reached the side of her porch, she crammed the notebook under her bare armpit and crouched near the wooden foundation, which was mostly hidden by an overgrown hydrangea bush. She pushed the branches away and revealed a part of the foundation that was missing a few slats. Natalie peered into the dark hole under the porch — it was about as wide as her shoulders. She knew that this hole led to a small crawl space, because there was a similar spot under her own porch. In fact, all of the houses on the block, each around eighty years old, were built like this. Natalie wasn't sure what the little space was used for in the past, and she certainly had never been in one. She always imagined them as dank, creepy places where raccoons and rats hid during the day.

As Annie crawled into the hole, Natalie made one last attempt to grab the notebook. It was as if Annie had eyes in the back of her head and could see Natalie reaching, because she flung the notebook through the shadowy opening.

"Hey!" Natalie protested. "Now it's going to be all dirty."

"If you mention the notebook again, I won't give it back," Annie said. "Understand?"

Natalie opened her mouth to argue, then bit her lips closed. Maybe it was best to stay quiet in the presence of a lunatic. Keep your mouth shut. Listen to this crazy girl's secret, rescue the notebook, go home. Nobody gets hurt.

Annie disappeared through the hole. Then she poked her head back out into the sunshine.

"No raccoons today," she said. "Come in."

No one will see me crawl into this hole, Natalie thought. No one will see this psychotic kid strangle me and leave my dead body to rot under her porch forever. *Ricky,* she prayed silently to her six-year-old brother, *if I die you can have my bike and my books.* She pulled the strap of her bike helmet a little tighter, then inched inside.

The moist, chilly dirt pressed into her hands and knees. The air inside was much cooler than outside, and it smelled earthy and damp. Once they were both in, Annie leaned a wooden board against the hole to block the light.

Natalie scanned the room for the notebook, but it was too dark to see anything. She was afraid to sit down. What if she sat on something dead? She took off her bike helmet and perched on it, her head brushing the low ceiling. Annie was busy rummaging in the corner, but in the dark, Natalie couldn't make out exactly what she was doing. Gradually her eyes began to adjust, and she saw thin seams of light overhead, where the sun was coming through cracks in the porch floor. Now she could tell that Annie was digging around in some kind of wooden crate.

"Get up for a second," she said. Natalie did her best to stand under the low ceiling, and Annie whipped open a folded blanket. A billow of musty air wafted in Natalie's direction.

"So you don't get your nice clothes dirty," Annie explained, motioning her to sit.

"Thanks," Natalie coughed. "But I'm fine sitting on my bike helmet. And anyway, these are just play clothes."

"Well, they're fancier than what I'm wearing," Annie said, slapping her bare chest. "Why were you using a helmet, anyway?"

"Because I was riding my bike."

"But you were just riding around the block."

"So?" Natalie said. "I want to be safe."

"Safe?" Annie gave her a blank look.

"I read a book once about a kid who didn't wear a bike helmet," Natalie explained. "He ended up in the hospital with a cracked skull."

"Do you read a lot?" Annie asked. "You seem like you read a lot." She said it as if she didn't think much of reading.

"Yeah. Don't you?"

Annie shrugged. "I'm not that good at it." She reached back into the crate.

"So what's the secret?" Natalie asked impatiently.

"Hold your horses," Annie said.

Natalie's eyes were used to the low light now. She watched Annie pull out a red matchbox and a fat, mostly used-up candle. Annie worked the candle stub into the dirt at the edge of the blanket. She then struck a match on the side of the little red box, as Natalie had only ever seen an adult do. The flame lit Annie's face from below, so it looked like a mask. Her eyes became black stones and her cheeks glowed bright. Natalie felt the light dancing on her own face, too. The flame was inching down the matchstick, closer and closer to Annie's grubby fingertips.

"You're going to burn yourself!" Natalie hissed.

"You're afraid of everything, aren't you?" Annie said. She touched the flame to the wick of the candle. It crackled to life and threw light on the old wooden floorboards above, against the short wooden walls, the ancient green army blanket, and Annie. It seemed like nighttime in a place far from home. It was hard to believe that outside was a bright summer day on the same old street.

Annie dug one hand into the dirt behind her, and pulled out two dingy gold coins, bigger than quarters. She held one in each hand for Natalie to see.

"What are those?" Natalie asked, reaching toward them. Annie pulled her hands back.

"Nuh-uh, can't touch 'em." She rubbed the dirt off the tops of the coins with her thumbs. "And if you knew what they were, you wouldn't want to touch anyway. These were on my dead mom's eyes."

"What?!" Natalie jumped, hitting her head on the porch floor above. She wished she'd left her bike helmet on. "Your mom is dead?"

Natalie didn't know anyone with a dead mom. She read books about orphans all the time — there were a million books starring orphans. But in real life? She couldn't think of anyone whose mom was actually dead. Natalie tried for a moment to imagine what it would be like if her mom wasn't alive, picking weeds in the garden or making lunch in the kitchen. Impossible.

"Yep. Died last year," Annie said matter-of-factly. "So she had these coins on her eyes —"

"Wait," Natalie interrupted. "If she was dead, how did she put those on her eyes?"

"My mom didn't put them on. The funeral director did." Annie covered her own eyes with the coins to demonstrate. "It's so no one would accidentally look into her eyes after she was dead. Because if you look into a dead person's eyes, you die too."

"Yeah, right," Natalie said. "I've never heard that before."

Annie lowered the coins. "Of course *you* haven't."

"What is that supposed to mean?" Natalie asked.

Annie shook her head and continued, "When you look into a dead person's eyes, it's like you're watching a little mini TV show of your life. There are scenes from when you were nice to people, and the rest is about how you were a jerk. Then you die a minute later. That's what it was like for me, anyway."

"Shouldn't you be dead now?" Natalie asked. This was getting ridiculous.

"Well, that's the thing," Annie said. "There's an exception to the Rule of the Dead Eye." She said the last part in a spooky vampire voice. "If you swallow the coins before the minute is up, you live."

"Aren't they a little big to swal —" Natalie started to say, but Annie cut her off.

"Just listen. My mom was lying in a casket at her funeral with these over her eyes." She held up the coins again. "They're dirty now, but at the time, they were really shiny."

Natalie imagined a dead lady with big, golden eyes. A shiver wriggled up her spine like an earthworm.

"After the service," Annie continued, "everyone went into the other room for cake and lemonade, but I stayed with Mom, because I wanted to see her one last time. I was looking at her, lying there in her best blue party dress with those big, fat coins over her eyes, and I missed her so much. I wanted to have something to remember her by." Annie's voice cracked. "I forgot for a minute about the Rule of the Dead Eye, and I did a really stupid thing: I reached over the side of the coffin and took the coins off her eyes. Suddenly, her eyes popped open like *this!*" She jerked her face toward Natalie's, her eyes bugged out like a zombie.

"AAAH!" Natalie jumped again, and banged her head on the porch floor for the second time. "OW!"

"Shhh!" Annie commanded. Natalie gave her a dirty look, then strapped on her bike helmet.

"Even though I wanted to look away, I couldn't," Annie said, her face striped with shadows. "It was like her eyes were magnets pulling me in, forcing me to look. And then this little movie came on in the dark centers of her eyes, and it started showing me my life. I saw when I was a baby, then I was two, then four, and I knew there wasn't a moment to lose. I put the coins in my mouth and ran into the reception room, to the table with cake and lemonade. I crammed a piece of cake in my mouth, to help me swallow the coins. Then I drank a cup of lemonade in one gulp to wash everything down. It spilled on my fancy dress and I had frosting all over my face, but I finally swallowed the whole mess. Everyone was looking at me like I was from outer space. I was worried someone would suspect something. But then this little old lady said, 'Poor girl misses her momma.' Everyone nodded and left me alone after that."

Annie began polishing one coin on the hem of her shorts. Natalie sat there in the flickering half-light, watching her. It was the most outrageous story she had heard in all her life. What a magnificently absurd lie. Since when do dead people show your personal home movies in their pupils? And if you tried to swallow something as big as those coins, you'd end up in the hospital.

Why would someone take something tragic like their mom dying, and make it worse with a ridiculous lie? Natalie had no idea how to respond.

After a long pause, she decided to say, "That's a cool story. But it seems sort of fake."

Annie sighed down at her lap, squeezing the coins in her tight fists. Natalie studied her face. *Is she mad now? Is she going to throw those coins at me?* Instead, Annie started crying.

"You think I'm a liar?" she asked, slow and sad. A sob escaped, and she brought her tear-filled eyes up to look at Natalie. "Why would I make up something so awful about my mom?" She shook her head and dropped the coins back into their little grave by the wall. "I mean, I know it's an amazing story, but to think it's not true . . ." A loud sniffle echoed in the underground room as Annie covered the coins with fistfuls of dirt.

Now Natalie really didn't know what to say. None of this made sense. First Annie showed her a dead bird, then stole her notebook, bullied Natalie into coming to this dank little room, told her a wild lie, and now she was crying.

Sometimes in fairy tales, being nice to the strangest, rudest creature turns it into a beautiful princess or handsome prince. The princess or prince then showers the kind person with gold or jewels or wishes. *If this was a fairy tale*, Natalie thought, *this would be the part where I decide whether or not I'm going to be nice to this crazy girl.* Natalie didn't believe Annie's story. But for a reason she couldn't quite name, Natalie wanted to be kind to her. There was something so different and strangely fascinating about her.

She reached for Annie's hand. "I'm really sorry your mom died," Natalie said.

Annie measured Natalie through squinted eyes, then took her outstretched hand. Grit pressed between their palms.

"So you believe me then? About my mom?" Annie asked. Before Natalie could answer, the floorboards above them creaked. Annie put a filthy finger to her lips. They heard the metal porch door twang shut, and heavy footsteps go into the house.

"My uncle Ralph," Annie whispered, pointing to the ceiling. "Home from work. He doesn't know about the coins."

"You live with your uncle?" Natalie asked. "Where's your dad?"

"I never met him," Annie said, her ear still tilted toward the ceiling. "He left my mom right after I was born."

"It sounds like he went inside," Natalie said. "But let's change the subject to be safe."

"I like black olives," Annie said out of nowhere.

"Really?" Natalie said. "Me too."

"Olive. That could be your code name for our secret-collecting club."

"What secret-collecting club?"

"Well, I'm just thinking," Annie said, "now we have two secrets, right?"

Natalie nodded. "The bird and the coins."

"There must be tons more," Annie said. "I bet everyone on our block has a secret. We could have a club to collect them. We'll find out everyone's business," she giggled. "Won't that be funny?"

"It actually sounds kind of rude," Natalie said.

"What, finding out the truth? That's not rude. That's what priests and policemen always tell you to do — to be truthful." Annie reached into a shadowy spot behind her and brought Natalie's notebook into the light.

"You can have this back now," she said, setting it in Natalie's lap. "I wasn't really going to keep it. I just wanted you to come see my secret."

"It's okay," Natalie said. "There are just old spelling tests in here." She brushed the dirt off the notebook cover and handed it back to Annie. "Actually, you can have it."

"Really?" Annie said. She cradled it as if it was a Miss America bouquet instead of a half-used-up notebook.

"Yeah. It's a present," Natalie said.

"Then I have a present for you." Annie rummaged in the crate in the corner again, and pulled out two candy bars. She handed one to Natalie.

"Thanks," Natalie said. She crinkled open the wrapper and took a polite nibble. "I've read books about spies, you know."

"Oh yeah?" Annie bit off a huge hunk of her candy bar.

"Yes, but they usually have good reasons for

spying. They're spying to save their country or family or something big like that."

Annie chewed her enormous mouthful thoughtfully.

"Well, we can spy to save ourselves from a boring summer," she said, then smiled. Her teeth were coated in chocolate. "And I don't know a lot of people on this street. It would be a good way to get to know them."

"I guess that's true, in a way," Natalie said. "But I doubt everyone on the block has a secret. Our neighbors are nice, but they're boring. They hang around their houses and mow their lawns."

"Don't be fooled by people who seem boring," Annie said. "Even the most dull-looking people do all kinds of weird, interesting things when they think no one's watching." Annie crammed the last of the candy in her mouth, wadded the empty wrapper and tossed it into a dark corner. "Now, your code name is Olive, but I need one too."

Natalie nodded, taking another dainty bite.

"A good code name is something nobody would

ever expect," Annie said. She bowed her head to her knees in a kind of yoga stretch. Then she sat up and looked at Natalie solemnly.

"From now on," Annie said, "you will call me Elvis."

"Elvis?" Natalie giggled. "You're joking." It came out before she had a chance to stop it. Annie shot her a look that could have melted Natalie's chocolate bar down the front of her shirt.

"You're not thinking like a spy," Annie said. "Don't you see it's better to have a totally random name? No one will ever guess it's me."

Annie was right. No one would make the connection between Elvis, the dead rock star, and this skinny blond girl. No one would ever guess that Elvis meant Annie. Genius. And for that matter, no one would suspect that Olive meant Natalie.

"Elvis." Natalie nodded.

"Olive," Annie said.

Then Annie spat on the candle, and the first meeting of their secret club was officially over.

Chapter Three

"Look at that lawn. It hasn't been mowed since they moved in," Natalie's mom said, pointing a forkful of pasta salad at Annie's house. The Wallis family was eating dinner on the porch that evening, because the breeze was so soft and cool.

Natalie's dad said, "Maybe they're waiting for it to grow into a jungle, so wild animals will move in and eat the grass down to the proper length."

"Grass? I don't see any grass," Natalie's mom said, squinting. "Just dandelions."

"Yep, only ugly dandelions," said Natalie's

little brother, Ricky. He held out his empty glass for more milk, and smiled at his sister. Natalie poured.

"Dandelions are kind of pretty," Natalie said. "The flowers look like little suns."

"Technically, sweetie, they're not flowers," her mom said. "They're weeds." As someone who tended a large garden in the backyard, her mom knew the difference.

Natalie's mom was tall and strikingly beautiful, with long blond hair like Barbie. But she was a lot smarter than Barbie. She worked from home as an accountant, helping people organize their money and pay taxes on time. Maybe because she looked so perfect, or because she had to find the one correct answer for every tax calculation, she felt there was just one perfect way to do everything. One right way to mow a lawn. To act around other people. To belong in the neighborhood.

Natalie's dad also liked to do things perfectly. He

was a pharmacist at the RexHealth drugstore four blocks away. He counted pills all day and poured them into tiny bottles. "There's only one medication for every prescription," he once told Natalie. "And one right number of pills." *Is that why they got married?* Natalie sometimes wondered. *Because they both like to count things?*

"They only moved in a month ago," Natalie pointed out. "Once they finish unpacking, they'll take care of the yard."

"Maybe." Her mom shrugged. "Hey missy, I almost forgot!" She set down her fork and squeezed Natalie's hand. "Your grades came in the mail today. A, A+, A, A. That's my smart girl!"

"Wow," her dad said. "That's great, Nat. Congratulations."

"Thanks," Natalie said, relieved the conversation topic had changed.

"What about me?" Ricky asked. "Aren't I smart?"

"You're very smart, honey," his mom said. "My

little architect! Did you start on your new project today?"

"Yep," Ricky said proudly. Ricky Wallis's favorite activity was building things. But he didn't build everyday objects like chairs or doors — he chose ambitious projects like pirate ships and skyscrapers. And he never drew up plans, because they were a waste of his time. He would simply nail pine boards together and hope things turned out. Natalie had seen his latest work in the driveway when she came in for dinner. It looked like the beginning of a slide, though the ramp was made of so many different boards that if people slid down it, they'd get splinters in their pants.

"I'm building a carnival for the block party," Ricky announced. "There's going to be a giant slide, a Ferris wheel, and maybe a roller coaster, if I have time. I had to stop working today because it got too hot."

"It was much too hot," Natalie's mom agreed. "Though that's no reason to run around outside without a shirt. Did you see that little girl today?" She nodded toward Annie's house.

"How could you tell she's a girl?" Natalie asked.

Her mom considered this. "She has a feminine face, I guess."

"What kind of parents let their girl run around half-naked?" her dad wondered. "Pass the salt, please."

"I met her today," Natalie said, handing him the saltshaker. "Her name is Annie. I thought she was a boy at first."

"I'd assume a kid without a shirt was a boy, too," her dad said.

"She doesn't live with her parents," Natalie said. "Her mom is dead, and she never knew her dad. She lives with her uncle."

"Oh my," Natalie's mom said, shaking her head. "She must be so mixed-up."

"I like her," Natalie said in Annie's defense. "I hope we'll be friends."

"That would be nice," Natalie's mom said, but she didn't sound as if she meant it. She pursed her lips tight for a moment, then said brightly, "Now, who wants dessert?"

Natalie lay in her bed that night, watching the wind breathe her curtains in and out of the window. She was thinking about Annie.

Annie wasn't like any of Natalie's friends from school. Her private-school friends were sweet, polite, pretty girls. At recess, they'd play fair, orderly games of four-square, in which everyone got their chance to be in the "A" spot. When Natalie had one of her friends over after school, they would both be so worried about being polite that they wouldn't ever get down to playing. They'd get stuck asking each other, "What do you want to do?"

"I don't know, what do you want to do?"

"I don't know, what do *you* want to do?"

"I don't *know*, what do *you* want to do?"

Eventually, one of them would suggest something like, "Do you want to play checkers?" Then the conversation would get stuck again:

"I want to if you want to."

"Well, I want to if *you* want to."

"But do you really want to? Let's do something else if you want to."

"Do you *want* to do something else?"

"I don't know, what do you want to do?"

Natalie and her guest would waste so much time deciding what to do that by the time they finally picked something, it was time for the friend to go home. It made Natalie want to scream. But that wouldn't be very polite.

Annie was not polite. She was bossy and rude, and she would probably rather sneak into the teacher's lounge at recess than play four-square. Her idea of fun was spying on the neighbors and pocketing dead birds. She didn't care if she wasn't wearing a shirt or had chocolate on her teeth. Annie was wild and tough, like an alley cat. She was mysterious and a little bit scary. Natalie never had any friends like that. Not until now.

She thought about Annie's story of those dead-eye coins. No way was it true. But if it wasn't true, why would she tell it? Maybe, Natalie thought, she invented a crazy story to make herself less sad about her mom. Like a story Band-Aid.

Natalie turned over onto her stomach and found the face on the headboard of her bed. It was really just a spot where the white paint was chipping away to the wood below. But it looked like the face of a woman with long hair and a slim, pointy nose. The profile of her head was tipped away slightly, as if she was waiting for someone to pour a secret in her ear. Natalie would sometimes whisper secrets to her, or tell her when she was mad or sad about something. She pretended this nice, long-haired woman was listening.

Natalie knew a headboard was a strange place to find a friend, but in the books she read, characters made friends in all kinds of weird locations: the middle of a blizzard, the cereal aisle of the grocery store, a rocking ship at sea. And most often, the stranger the place, the stronger the bond. So even though Natalie was very different from Annie, the fact that their friendship began in a dark, gritty crawl space beneath a porch gave her hope.

She leaned so close to the paint-chip lady, her lips nearly brushed the headboard. *Maybe Natalie wouldn't be friends with Annie,* she confessed. *But Olive can be friends with Elvis.*

Chapter Four

When Natalie was riding her bike that first day of summer, the day she met Annie, she was trying to beat her best time around the block. That was the main reason. But in the back of her mind she also had a small, private wish she hardly wanted to admit was there. Natalie hoped she would catch a glimpse of Steven Redding, the sweetest, cutest boy in the whole school. The boy she had secretly liked for three years.

Steven lived six houses down and waited at the same bus stop as Natalie. He was twelve — a year and a half older than her. He had black hair and warm brown eyes with extra-long eyelashes. His mouth turned up more on one side, which made him look adorable and sneaky at the same time.

Steven's face had only one imperfection: a tiny crescent-shaped scar near his left eye. Natalie had stared at it for ten minutes once on the bus ride home, while he read a comic book. She watched him mouth the words and laugh quietly at the good parts, and her crush deepened like a heart you trace over and over on your notebook cover.

Natalie knew that a lot of other girls at school liked Steven Redding, girls his age who were allowed to wear lip gloss, had pierced ears, and weren't too shy to say hi to him. Girls who made sure they laughed loudly near Steven, to seem popular and fun. But Natalie was glad because during the summer, Steven wouldn't see those girls from school. He'd hang around the neighborhood and just see her.

Natalie wished she could work up the courage to say hi, instead of ignoring him as she usually did when they waited at the bus stop. If only he would smile that crooked smile right at her.

As she biked around the block on the first day of summer, Natalie stole glances at Steven Redding's house. She imagined that he might come out to sit on the front stoop, and admire the way she skillfully rounded the corner or avoided a particularly nasty crack in the sidewalk. Or he'd say, "Hey! I used to have that same bike, only it was blue!" This would lead to a half-hour conversation, and he'd offer her a piece of gum, warm from his pocket, before he said good-bye. Or even better, she would wobble on her bike as he approached, and fall and skin her knee. Steven would race to her and say, "Oh my god! Are you okay? Let me get you a Band-Aid. Hey, this is a good time to say that I've always had a crush on you. . . ."

It happened in the stories Natalie read all the time. Why couldn't it happen for real?

Because I'm just Natalie, she thought. This would probably be like last summer, when every time she saw

Steven she'd stop whatever she was doing and stand there, frozen like a statue.

Last summer she would always see him walking to the park pool two blocks away, his younger brother Noah by his side. Noah was her age, and had been in her third- and fourth-grade classrooms. He always made a point of sitting next to her during reading. Noah liked Natalie, but Natalie didn't like him back. There was a good reason why.

Noah tortured bugs. Natalie would sometimes see him sitting on his front walk, coloring big black ants with sidewalk chalk. He'd brush the chalk against the ant's back, let it walk around a little with its fashionable new look, then squish it. One time at the bus stop, Noah showed Natalie a daddy longlegs with all the legs pulled off. It was just a sad brown ball.

Natalie now sat on her bed, tying her tennis shoes. It was the second day of summer break, and the morning sun was slanting in through her window. She was getting ready to go see Annie and have another club meeting. As she pulled her laces tight, Natalie realized something fantastic. Since she was in a secret-collecting club now, she finally had a way to be around Steven. Of course, he wouldn't know she was around, because she'd be spying on him. She could learn all kinds of stuff about him, more than his friends even knew. Natalie might discover his favorite kind of food, then show up one day at his house with a plate of it.

She'd say, "Hi. My name is Natalie, and I live six houses away. We go to the same bus stop, but I've never actually met you. What's your name? Stewart? Stefan? Oh, *Steven*, that's right. Anyway, I made a ton of these fudge brownies, and I can never eat them all. Want some?" Then he would invite her into his house and they would watch TV together all day. Or she'd find out his favorite kind of music, and play it really loud from her bedroom every day until he came to her door, asking, "Who is playing that cool music? I must meet her!"

While Natalie was lost in her daydreams, she had knotted her shoelace five times. It was so tight, she'd probably have to cut it when she wanted to take her shoes off. *Or,* she thought, *I could ask Steven to untie it. I bet he's good at untying knots.* He seemed good at everything.

"I'm going to play with Annie today," Natalie announced at breakfast. She always told her parents if she was going out — it was a rule.

"Who's Annie?" Ricky asked. His hammer sat on the table beside his cereal spoon. "Does she want to help me build my carnival?"

"Annie is the new girl on the block," Natalie's dad reminded Ricky. He filled four glasses with precisely the same amount of orange juice, then passed one to each person.

"I think we're going to do our own stuff, Rick," Natalie said. "You go ahead with your carnival."

"Wouldn't you rather invite over a friend from school?" her mom asked. "I could pick her up." She spooned up a delicate bite of oatmeal.

"No, that's okay. Annie and I made plans."

"So what are you two up to?" her dad asked.

"Oh, nothing really," Natalie said. She didn't want to give details or lie, so she excused herself from the table. "I better go. She's probably waiting for me." She took her blue backpack from the arm of the chair and slung it over her shoulder.

"Want some breakfast before you leave?" her dad asked.

"I'll take a slice of toast," she said, reaching for the plate.

"Have fun, sweetie," her mom said. She was wearing the same tight, worried smile from yesterday. Like she wished her daughter was meeting a pleasant, polite friend from school instead of a weird, barechested girl.

"I have to leave for work," her dad said, pushing his chair back from the table.

"And I'm going to get started on the garden," Natalie's mom said, flipping on a pair of sunglasses. "If I don't get my tomato plants in the ground today, they'll wilt."

"Okay," Natalie said. "Have fun planting." She bit into her toast and went out the front door.

Natalie's house was one of the most impressive on the block. It was two-and-a-half stories tall, with a fresh coat of blue paint that complemented the white front porch. The wide wooden steps were decorated with tidy, fragrant pots of geraniums and lavender, and the miniature pine trees on either side of the front door were groomed into neat, even cones. It was the kind of house you'd see in a magazine.

Natalie headed toward Annie's house, across the street and one door over. It was the exact opposite of Natalie's, being the smallest on the block and the most run-down. The previous owners moved out two years ago, and it had not been cared for since then.

The ancient wooden siding had shed most of its gray paint, and the boards were warping away from the walls, trying to escape from the ugliness. The screen door had a huge dent near the bottom where someone had given it a good kick. There was no garden, and not any grass, either. Just a tangle of dandelions gone to seed.

Annie was sitting on her front steps, cooling her face with a homemade paper fan. She had what seemed to be a tablecloth tied around her waist like a skirt. And same as yesterday, no shirt. Natalie waved to her as she came up Annie's sidewalk.

Before they could say hello, Natalie heard the burbled spray of a garden hose. Both girls turned to see Ms. Hatch, Annie's next-door neighbor, watering the flowers along the side of her house. The woman looked up and waved at the girls.

Ms. Hatch was sixty-nine years old and lived alone. When she wasn't working in her garden, she was making clay pots and vases. She used to sell her pottery to gift shops, but her hands had grown shaky with age, and everything she made now came out crooked. So she had pots and more pots that no one ever bought, and she set them around her backyard. Natalie went to Ms. Hatch's with her mom once, to dig up some lilies that the old woman wanted to thin out. Her yard looked like a strange, pottery-only garage sale, with vases and pots all over her windowsills and deck and along the brick path to her back door. Some of the pottery was filled with animal nests, and the rest held rainwater.

Ms. Hatch set the hose on the grass and walked over. "Hello, girls," she said, pulling off her gardening gloves. "What a pretty day!"

"Hi, Ms. Hatch," Natalie said. For some reason, she felt embarrassed to be seen with Annie. Would it kill her to put on a shirt? She felt guilty for thinking this. "Have you met Annie? She moved in this spring."

"Oh yes, we've met. So nice to see you again," Ms. Hatch said. She bent down to where Annie was sitting and took up a corner of her makeshift skirt. "My, is this a tablecloth you're wearing? What a wonderful idea! It's so colorful," she said. "You have an artistic streak — I can tell. We artists think alike." She and Annie shared a smile.

A puddle widened on the sidewalk.

"Oops!" Ms. Hatch said. "I better get back to my watering before I make a swimming pool in your yard." She winked at the girls, picked up the hose, and disappeared around the side of her house.

"I like her," Annie said. "She's the only one besides you who's nice. Everyone else whispers about me. Or laughs out loud." Natalie thought of the kids at her bus stop.

Without another word, Annie waved her fan toward the side of her house. Natalie nodded. Once inside their headquarters, Annie lit the candle.

"Elvis, I brought something for our club," Natalie said, unzipping her backpack. She reached inside and drew out a package of colorful pushpins and a neat stack of note cards, the kind her mom used to copy recipes from TV cooking shows.

"See, we can write people's secrets on these, and tack them to the walls in here." She held a card up to the shadowy wooden wall to demonstrate.

"That's a great idea, Olive," Annie said. "It'll be like a little art exhibit of secrets. Or secret wallpaper."

"Look what else I brought." She pulled out a plastic baggie of sunflower seeds. "In case we get hungry."

Annie eyed the gray seeds skeptically.

"I'd have to be pretty hungry to eat those. What else you got?"

Natalie unzipped the front pocket and pulled out a pink pencil covered in iridescent hearts. It had a few chew marks, but Natalie had at least sharpened it into a nice new point. Annie grabbed the pencil and scowled at it in the candlelight.

"Pink?" she said, "I hate pink." She stabbed the pencil point into the dirt.

"Well, I love pink," Natalie said, gingerly pulling it out by the eraser. "And we needed something to write the cards with."

"I'll use that ugly pencil on one condition," Annie said. "That we don't take it out of our headquarters. I couldn't bear to see that pink in daylight."

"Fine with me," Natalie said. "*Headquarters*. I love that word. You know, our headquarters is just perfect. I really love this headquarters. We couldn't have found a better headquarters for our club."

Annie rolled her eyes. "If you say that word one more time, you owe me a dollar." Then she announced, "Olive, I propose we have a secret pledge."

"That would be good, Elvis," Natalie agreed.

"It has to be official, so we should swear on something," Annie said, looking around.

"The secret note cards?" Natalie suggested.

"Not serious enough. Oh, I know. It's perfect." Annie pulled the dead bird out of a fold in her skirt. It looked a little worse than yesterday. "We'll swear on this."

"Uh. Gross," Natalie said, wincing. "I'm not touching that."

"No. Just hold your hand above it, like this. There. Now repeat after me: I solemnly swear that I will do my best to find out all the secrets of this neighborhood, share them with the secret club members, and record them on the secret note cards. If I don't, may Annie's mom rise up and haunt me forever," Annie vowed.

". . . haunt me forever," Natalie finished a few seconds later, her eyes closed so she wouldn't have to see the decomposing bird.

"Now we'll bury the secret swear bird here." Annie used her free hand to widen the hole she'd made with the pencil point. She set the bird ceremoniously inside the hole, swept dirt over the top, and tamped it down with her heel.

"Good-bye, little bird," Natalie whispered. "Amen."

"You think that bird is still around?" Annie asked, brushing off her heel. "His spirit's already in heaven, sitting on my mom's shoulder. Don't you worry about him." When she mentioned her mom, Natalie's stomach flip-flopped. Annie's lie from yesterday wiggled in her belly like a freshly caught fish.

With the same hand that had buried the bird, Annie reached into the bag of sunflower seeds. She scooped out a handful and tossed it far back into her mouth. Her face twisted in disgust. "These are awful," she said, spitting the half-chewed bits onto the floor. "Try them."

Natalie looked into the baggie, which now had crumbs of bird-infested dirt clinging to the sides. "No thanks," she said. "You can have all of them."

"Ugh. No way." Annie cleaned her palms on her bare chest. Natalie cringed at what she knew she had to say.

"As long as we're proposing things," she announced, "I propose that spies wear shirts." She pinched her eyes shut and waited for Annie to say something nasty. Or hurl a handful of dirt in her face. From what Natalie knew so far, Annie was unpredictable.

But Annie just shrugged and said, "Okay."

"Great," Natalie said with relief.

"Enough talk, Olive. Let's go out and do some spying."

"What, now?" Natalie asked. "As in today, right this minute?"

"Yes, *now*," Annie said. "Just let me grab a shirt."

When they were talking about spying on their neighbors, Natalie had imagined it happening in the distant future, when she would somehow feel ready. But maybe she wouldn't feel ready to spy tomorrow, or the next day, or even next year. Might as well start now.

"Okay. Yeah. Let's go," Natalie said with growing conviction. She spat on the candle to end the meeting, and Annie clapped.

"Wow!" Annie said into the fresh darkness, "Miss Perfect is learning to spit!"

Chapter Five

Annie suggested that they spy on the big, green house two doors down from hers. They camped out under the kitchen window and peered inside for signs of the young couple Natalie knew lived there. The woman was pregnant, and Annie wanted to see how she managed to wash dishes with her enormous belly pressing against the sink. But no one was home except for a big, black dog. After spying on the dog for ten minutes, all he did was drink from his water dish and lie down on the sunny kitchen linoleum.

"What should we do now?" Natalie asked. "We could spy on Ms. Hatch."

"Nah," Annie said.

"We could peek in the house next to mine. It's for sale and the last owners already moved out."

Annie wrinkled her nose. "I don't want to spy on another empty house. Let's go down the alley."

Natalie and Annie cut through the pregnant lady's backyard into the alley, and began walking past the backs of the houses. Natalie was used to the fronts of the houses from riding her bike around the block. Seeing the backs was weird. They were all the same colors as the fronts, but with new details like gardens and decks and barbecue grills.

As they headed to the other end of the block, they passed the backs of the houses belonging to Virginia Brooks, the Warsaws, and Mr. Gonzales. At Mr. Gonzales's house, Annie stopped and gasped. She pointed excitedly toward a garage on the opposite side of the alley, at a couple of cardboard boxes sitting by the trash cans.

"Look! Free stuff!" she cried. She rushed to the

biggest box, which came to her waist, and started digging.

"How do you know it's free?" Natalie asked, watching the back door anxiously. Mr. Gonzales had been Natalie's third-grade teacher. She hoped he wouldn't see her, his A+ student, hanging out in the alley near a box of garbage.

"Because it says right here, 'Free — please take,'" Annie said, slapping one of the box flaps. "Ooh, look at this, Olive!" She withdrew a heavy piece of blue fabric from the pile and held her arm up as high as she could, but still the material brushed the ground.

"What is that?" Natalie asked, her embarrassment turning into curiosity. She pulled one edge of the fabric so it fanned out wide. "Oh, I know. It's a choir robe." Natalie pointed to the center of the fabric. "See the zipper in front?"

"Cool," Annie said. "Gimme." She found the opening at the bottom of the gown and heaved it over her head. First Annie's hands emerged from the massive sleeves, and then her head came through the neck hole. Annie centered the wide V-neck and smoothed the tiny front pleats.

"Man, I'm never taking this off," she said.

"Are you sure you should wear that?" Natalie asked. She pointed at the back door of the house. "What if someone comes out and sees?"

"They'll probably be thrilled we're taking this junk off their hands. Now, what else is in here . . . ?" Annie's voice became an echo as she leaned back into the box.

"Are there any books?" Natalie asked.

"Oh, so now you're interested?" Annie teased. She stood up, her legs ending in a puddle of blue fabric. "Let's say this is a magic box, and it has anything you want inside it. What would you wish for?"

Natalie squatted down and picked at a weed growing through a crack in the concrete.

"Hmm. Anything I want?" She squinted up at Annie, who was just a silhouette against the bright sun.

"Yes!" Annie boomed, holding her arms out wide.

"Just tell me your heart's desire and I, Sir Elvis the Magnificent, will pull it out of my amazing, fantastic, enchanted cardboard box."

Natalie stripped the vein from a dandelion leaf as she considered the offer. *I want Steven Redding to like me. I want to be brave like Annie.* But these weren't things you could pull out of a box.

"I'll take a pair of red cowboy boots," she said, finally.

Annie bowed to Natalie.

"As you wish, my dear Olive."

Natalie stood up and curtsied. "Why thank you, Elvis."

Annie rolled one sleeve up to her armpit and reached far into the box, grimacing as she pushed her way through the pile. She bit her lip as she felt around, and suddenly she gasped. Natalie rushed over to her.

"What's wrong?" she asked. She expected Annie to say that her hand was stuck in a mousetrap, or that a raccoon was biting her fingers.

"Move this other stuff!" Annie yelped. Natalie grabbed an armload of pea-green bedsheets and dumped them onto the ground. Annie grunted as she tugged her arm up, and Natalie almost fell over when she saw what her friend was holding. A pair of pink cowboy boots.

"Oh my gosh," Natalie said.

Annie examined the boots, peering inside first and then checking the soles.

"Well," she said in a disappointed tone. "They're not the right color. And they look a little small for you. Here, try them on." Natalie pried off her tennis shoes. She was speechless as she slipped her right foot into a boot. The leather was stiff and her toes squeezed slightly against the pointed tip, but it fit. She put on the other one and looked down at the boots, amazed. She felt like Cinderella in her magic glass slippers. Annie clapped.

"They *are* the right size! And you like pink, right? Did you mean to say pink when you made your wish?"

"If I knew I would actually get what I asked for, I would've asked for something better," Natalie said. "Elvis, this is really creepy."

"I'm psychic," Annie said, shrugging. "My mom was psychic, too."

"Psychic doesn't mean you can make things appear out of nowhere. It means you know things before they happen," Natalie argued.

"Well, you're the one that asked for the boots. Maybe *you're* psychic. Maybe you predicted there were boots in that box." Annie bunched up the bottom of her robe and slung it over one arm. She started walking back toward their end of the block, motioning for Natalie to follow.

"Don't you want to know how this happened, Elvis?" Natalie said. "Don't you think it's weird?"

"Doesn't anything weird ever happen in those books you read?" Annie asked. She walked backward down the alley so she could look at Natalie. "Man, it's like you don't think anything good should happen to you. You got your wish. Be happy!"

Annie turned back around and kept walking, the sleeves of the robe swinging with each step. She didn't slow her pace, and Natalie couldn't run to catch up because the boots were too stiff.

As she walked home alone, Natalie had time to think. *Maybe it was just a coincidence. I asked for red, anyhow. If it was real magic, they would've come out red. And there was a ton of stuff in that box, so it isn't that strange that there would be a pair of cowboy boots, is it? But what if it was magic? Shoot. I should've asked for Steven to like me.*

Chapter Six

"O live! Get over here."

"What can you see?"

"Chicken. Come see for yourself," Annie whispered, beckoning Natalie over to the basement window with a robed arm. Natalie pushed her way out of the bush she'd been hiding in. She crawled on all fours to the window, careful not to scrape the tops of her new pink boots. The small window looked into the basement belonging to Robert Dewey, the army sergeant. Sergeant Dewey was about fifty years old and lived alone in the green and white house two doors down from Natalie.

Sergeant Dewey fought in a big war a long time ago, and he did such a great job that they let him train the younger soldiers now. He went away for weeks at a time on training missions, and his house stood empty until he came back. When he was home, Sergeant Dewey lifted dumbbells every day out in his backyard, and the metallic clank of one weight hitting the other echoed down the block. Natalie was glad Sergeant Dewey was out of town now, so there was no chance he would discover them peeking into his basement. If he did catch them, he'd probably give them a strange army punishment, like doing fifty one-armed push-ups or scrubbing his driveway with a toothbrush.

A striped curtain covered the basement window from the inside. But through a slit in the fabric, the girls saw what seemed to be a big blue balloon suspended from a hook in the ceiling.

"What is that supposed to be?" Annie asked. They both stared for a few seconds.

"It's a hot air balloon," Natalie said with a note of satisfaction. "Look at the little basket on the bottom."

"It's pretty small to be a hot air balloon. It couldn't give a ride to anything bigger than a hamster."

"A cat could fit in that basket."

"Well, it would feel cramped the whole ride," Annie argued.

"But look, it's just a model," Natalie said. "A real balloon would be deflated unless there was air pumping into it. That one must be made of papier-mâché or something."

"Yeah, you're right. The sides look kind of hard."

"Why would he build that?" Natalie wondered. "I mean, he's an army sergeant. He knows how to shoot a gun and capture enemy forces and stuff. Why would he make a model of a hot air balloon?"

"I would say that it's a present for someone," Annie said, "except he probably won't be able to get it out of his basement. It's too big to fit up the stairs."

"Maybe it's a present to himself," Natalie said with growing excitement. "Elvis, it's his hobby."

"His *secret* hobby, Olive," Annie said, her eyebrows raised. "You think his army buddies know about this? If you're a tough guy, you pick hobbies like fishing or hunting or spitting. You don't make papier-mâché balloons. Trust me, this is his secret."

"This is one to stick on the headquarters wall," Natalie said, smiling.

Trina George was fourteen years old and devastatingly beautiful. She lived with her parents in the white house next to Steven Redding's. During the summer, she would carry a lounge chair and a fashion magazine out onto her front lawn. She'd lie there all day in her bikini, tanning, flipping through her magazine, and sipping can after can of diet soda. She wore headphones and bopped her head to the music, ignoring everybody who walked by.

Trina hadn't always been snotty. It started last

winter, when her picture was in *Teen Town* magazine. In the photo, Trina was lying on a big canopy bed in a nightgown, talking on a pink telephone and smiling her perfect, glossy smile. Since the magazine came out, Trina was constantly making a pouting model face, in case a fashion photographer or talent scout happened to pass her front lawn.

Trina's mom made sure every house on the block got a free copy of the magazine featuring her gorgeous, talented daughter. Natalie had carefully torn out Trina's picture and kept it in her bottom desk drawer. She took it out sometimes, to try to find something that was even a little bit wrong with Trina. Like a tiny pimple or a crooked tooth or a hangnail. She never could.

Whenever Natalie biked past her, Trina never looked up from her lounger with a wave or a smile or even a blank stare. Either she couldn't hear over her music, or she simply thought Natalie wasn't cool enough to acknowledge.

Annie and Natalie sat on the curb across the

street from Trina's house. They were spying on her, but Annie said it was unnecessary to hide in a bush or behind a parked car. Beautiful people are used to being stared at for long periods of time, she explained.

"She'll just assume we're adoring fans. If she even notices us."

"Do you think she'll notice if I take notes about her?" Natalie asked, holding up a fresh note card and a pencil.

"Heck no. She'll think you're writing an article about her for a movie star magazine. Or working up the courage to beg for an autograph."

Trina was lying on her back, eyes closed, her magazine tossed carelessly onto the grass. The way her perfectly bronzed limbs were posed on the lounger, the sun hitting her golden hair — it seemed like a sunscreen ad.

"Do you want to look like her when you get older?" Annie asked.

"Ha," Natalie said. "I wish. But I don't think it will happen." She clasped her plain brown braids. "Do *you* want to look like her?"

"I probably will look like her," Annie said, making a face. "And I'll hate it. Her beauty is so boring."

"All the boys like it," Natalie said.

"So what?"

Steven's front door opened. He and Noah stepped out into the sun, beach towels around their necks. Natalie's heart quickened.

"Going to the park pool," Annie commented. "The swim twins."

"Yeah," Natalie agreed, trying to keep the nervous shake out of her voice.

"But who goes swimming in jeans?" Annie asked, pointing at Noah's pants.

"He wears those everywhere, all the time," Natalie said. "In fact, I've never seen Noah not wearing those jeans." He wore them from the first day of school to the last, whether it was hot or cold, rain or shine.

Despite getting so much use, Noah's jeans were always stiff and extra-dark blue, as if his mom bought them yesterday. When he walked, they made a peculiar *fip-fip-fip* sound as the inseams rubbed together.

Noah waved at Natalie, and she gave him an irritated, one-second wave in return. Steven didn't see Natalie because he was staring at Trina on her lounger. Trina, of course, showed no signs of noticing Steven. He kept staring long after he had passed her, so his head turned farther and farther back on his neck. Then he tripped on a crack in the sidewalk.

"Whoa," he stuttered. Noah caught his arm and they continued walking toward the park.

Natalie hoped his "whoa" was about the crack, not Trina.

Annie and Natalie agreed that before their next club meeting, they would each look for secrets on their own. "Divide and conquer," Annie said. That's the way they'd get the most secrets. When they met under the porch again, they would share what they had found out.

Natalie wanted her first solo spy mission to be Steven, of course. But when she thought about actually going over to his house and sneaking around the yard, her stomach twisted into a sour knot. *Maybe next week*, she told herself. For now Natalie chose an easier subject: Ricky.

It wasn't difficult to discover one of his secrets. The hardest part was that her mom came into the room while Natalie was spying, and started changing the sheets on Ricky's bed. Natalie had to pretend she was looking for a lost book.

"Where did you get those pink boots?" her mom asked. "I don't remember them."

"Annie gave them to me," Natalie said, peering under the bed.

"Oh. And how are things going with Annie?" Her mom pulled off a dirty pillowcase. "You're spending a lot of time with her."

"Isn't that okay?" Natalie asked. "We're staying in the neighborhood."

"I know," her mom said. "I just thought you might like to see your school friends for a change."

"They all have lots of other friends," Natalie said. "Annie only has me."

Her mom nodded, her lips pressed into a thin line. She kept smoothing the pillowcase over and over until there were absolutely no creases.

Natalie skipped across the street to Annie's porch and rapped on the piece of wood, which Annie had already put over the hole from the inside. After a moment, the panel slid away and Natalie crawled in. The candle was lit, and Annie was waiting on the blanket with two small bags of potato chips, the stack of note cards, and the pink pencil. Natalie barely had a chance to sit down.

"Let's hear yours first, Olive," Annie demanded.

"Geez. Hello to you too," Natalie said. "Okay, you know my little brother, Ricky?"

"I've seen him in your yard," Annie said, nodding. "Builder boy." Her pencil hovered over the note card like a bee ready to sting.

"Right. I was in my brother's room yesterday, and I found out one of his big secrets." Natalie paused for a good two seconds in hopes of building suspense. Annie scratched her nose without taking her eyes off Natalie.

"So? What was it?" Annie whispered.

"Ricky throws used tissues behind his bed," Natalie said, barely able to contain her giggles. "There's about a hundred of them. It's disgusting."

"Big deal," Annie said, tossing the note card and pencil to the blanket in disgust. "Your brother's practically a baby. I bet he doesn't even care if anyone knows he does that. Look, Olive, I'm not trying to be mean, but if this is going to be a great secret club, we have to get great secrets."

"I do have one more," Natalie offered. "But it's about people in my house again."

Annie reluctantly picked up the note card and pencil. "This better be good," she said.

"My mom and I went grocery shopping yesterday, and on the way home she wanted to stop at another store. But she said she'd only stop if I promised to keep quiet about what she bought."

"Okay," Annie said, scribbling. Her handwriting was loopy and messy, like tangled hair. "And?"

"So I promised I wouldn't tell, and she stopped at a place that sells old movies. She bought a Three Stooges film for my dad's birthday tomorrow. In this one, they work in a pharmacy, so my dad's going to love it."

"You're in a powerful position, Olive," Annie said. "You could totally ruin the surprise and say, 'Know what, Dad? You're getting a Three Stooges movie for your birthday.'"

"Why would I do that?" Natalie asked. She picked up a bag of chips and ripped open the seal.

"I'm just saying you *could*," Annie said, taking a chip from Natalie's bag. "Or every so often, you could whisper 'LarryCurlyMoe' real fast, so he wouldn't be sure he even heard it."

"I'm not going to do that," Natalie said. "It's supposed to be a *surprise*."

"I was in a movie once, you know."

"Really?" Natalie asked, crunching a large chip. "What movie?"

"It's called *Under the Cocoa Tree*."

"Never heard of it," Natalie said.

Annie fixed her with a pitiful look. "Is it my fault you don't watch French movies?"

Natalie frowned. *Another lie*. "All right, Elvis, let's hear *your* great secret then." She brushed oily chip crumbs off her hands and reached for the note cards and pencil.

"You know the peach-colored house in the middle of the block?" Annie asked.

"The one with the white metal awning." Natalie started writing. "That's Virginia Brooks. She used to be on TV, like, twenty years ago."

"Hey, I thought she looked familiar. That old detective show, right?"

"She was the secretary," Natalie said, nodding.

"Yeah, that's it," Annie said. "Around ten o'clock last night I peeked in her window."

"Ten o'clock?" Natalie squeaked, her pencil frozen in midair. "I have to be in bed by eight-thirty."

"I don't have a bedtime," Annie said, shrugging. "Anyway, there was Virginia, sitting at her vanity table. She was taking off her earrings and rings and stuff and getting ready for bed. Pretty normal, right? She opens up this jar of face cream and starts dabbing it around her eyes." Annie imitated Virginia's delicate gesture with her pinkies. "But then, she got a big gob on one finger and she ate it, like suddenly it's ice cream instead of face cream."

"Weird," Natalie said as she wrote. "And gross."

"Like I told you. People do weird things when they think no one's looking," Annie said.

"But what makes that secret so much better than the one about Ricky?" Natalie challenged. "How is eating face cream different from throwing used tissues behind your bed?"

"Isn't it obvious, Olive?" Annie asked. "It's the risk. It didn't take any guts to go look in your own brother's room. If someone comes in, you can make up a reason why you're in there. But if you're spying through some stranger's window and you get caught, there's no explanation."

Annie had a point. The spies in Natalie's books were always putting themselves in great peril to find out what they needed to know. Spies had to be brave.

"You're right, Elvis," Natalie nodded. "From now on, I'll take more risks."

Chapter Seven

Natalie knocked on Annie's screen door and a shadow approached from the dark living room. As the shadow reached the porch, it turned into a skinny woman with long black hair, long red fingernails, and a long, droopy face. She had a lot of makeup on, but it looked as if it was applied sometime last week and had been slowly smearing away since then. A cigarette hung from her waxy red lips.

"Whaddya want?" she said in a tired voice.

"Is Annie here?" Natalie asked. The lady didn't say anything, she simply turned around and shuffled back inside. Natalie was wondering if she would ever return when an earsplitting "Annie!" was shouted inside. She heard a loud clomping down the stairs, then Annie appeared in the doorway.

"Hey," she said, breathless.

Natalie nodded hello but kept her eyes on the woman in the darkness behind Annie. The woman collapsed into a brown recliner, the fabric sending out a wheeze of dust as she landed.

"Who is that?" Natalie whispered through the screen. "Is she okay?"

Annie rolled her eyes. "That's Charla, my uncle's new girlfriend. And no, she's not okay — she's annoying. Do you want some lemonade?"

"Sure," Natalie said. She didn't budge from the doorway.

"You have to come inside," Annie said, opening the door. "Did you think I was going to bring it to you? Like a waiter?"

"Should I take off my shoes?" Natalie asked.

Annie looked at her as if she was crazy. "Just come in already."

Natalie slipped off her pink cowboy boots anyway and walked into the living room. She'd never been inside Annie's house. The sun was already midway up the sky, but the heavy, orange curtains were all closed, blocking out the light. It smelled of cigarettes and deli ham in there. Natalie always found it funny to smell other people's houses. Some smelled like laundry, some like lemon cookies or cat pee. This one smelled like smoke and ham.

A wooden coffee table in the center of the living room was scattered with tabloid magazines from the grocery store, the ones about alien invaders and babies born with two heads. Next to the magazines was the deadest plant Natalie had ever seen — she guessed it had choked to death with all the smoke. Beside the plant was an ashtray holding a lit cigarette. The tip was sending up a wispy smoke signal, warning Natalie to go no further. *Watch out*, it said. *More bad smells ahead.*

"Look, Charla's out again," Annie said, pointing at the woman slumped in the reclining chair.

"She's asleep already? But she just answered the door."

"She and my uncle Ralph were out late last night," Annie said. "They hung out at the bar where he works."

"Does she live with you?" Natalie asked.

"Technically, no. But she's stayed over every night since Ralph met her a couple of weeks ago at the bar. Watch this," she said, and swaggered over to Charla's collapsed form. Annie reached into the pocket of Charla's bathrobe and pulled out a pack of cigarettes. Natalie had never actually seen a pack up close, just high on the rack at the gas station or on TV.

"Elvis, do you really think you should do that?" Natalie cringed.

"Believe me," Annie said, "a fire engine could drive through the front door, and she wouldn't wake up." To prove it, she stomped over to the couch as loudly as she could manage with bare feet, and lifted one of the cushions with gusto. There against the springs were at least ten flattened cigarette packs.

"Did you put those there?" Natalie asked in disbelief.

"Yep," Annie replied coolly, and tossed the pack she was holding onto the pile. Then she dropped the cushion back on top, and sealed her ritual with a few exuberant bounces on the seat, and a grin.

"It's so funny when she wakes up and goes, 'Where's my cigs? I swear I had some cigs.'" Annie patted invisible pockets on her chest and legs. Charla snorted in her sleep and mumbled, "Mmmn . . . turn left . . . hey . . . Hershey's chocolate."

Natalie shot Annie a worried look.

"She's out cold," Annie assured her. "Charla always babbles in her sleep. Let's get that lemonade."

Natalie followed Annie, who was wearing a yellow bathing suit, into the kitchen.

"Are you going swimming?" Natalie asked.

"No. I ran out of clean underwear. And it's too hot for that choir robe. Hey, do you know Albert Castle?" Annie was filling a plastic pitcher with tap water.

"Is that the tall guy who lives next door to you?" Natalie asked.

"Yeah." Annie removed the plastic scoop from a can of powdered pink lemonade and poured most of the can into the pitcher.

"My mom says his house is too big for just one person," Natalie said.

"It's actually not, since he's so tall. He has to be careful not to hit his head in the doorways," Annie said. She stirred the lemonade with a butter knife, then poured out two big glasses. "Let's go up to my room and wait for him to come home from work. He does something really funny right when he walks in the door."

"Okay." Natalie pretended it wasn't a big deal to go up to Annie's room, but it was. She couldn't imagine what it looked like. Natalie was careful not to spill the lemonade as she climbed the steps, although the threadbare green carpet probably wouldn't have minded. In a room at the top of the stairs, a man with a tired, freckled face sat on the bed, pulling off his dusty black boots. He looked confused when he saw Annie and Natalie standing there. Natalie felt awkward, as if invading a private moment.

"Natalie, this is my uncle Ralph," Annie said. "Ralph, this is Natalie. She lives across the street."

"How you doin'," Ralph said. His smile was wide but stiff.

"Good, thanks," Natalie said, and Annie pulled her into another bedroom, not much bigger than a closet. Two mattresses were stacked on the floor, covered with a sheet. The sheet was white with a pattern of tiny blue petals so faded, they were like the ghosts of flowers.

Pictures were drawn all over the white plaster of Annie's walls. Natalie followed the crayon, pencil, and marker mural around the room. There was a dense forest, a waterfall, and horses trotting through a field of flowers. There was a mountain range, and standing on the highest peak, a naked princess holding a wand.

"Did you draw all that?" Natalie asked. "It's really good."

"Thanks. I ran out of room, though. I need to get the step stool from the kitchen so I can do the high part." Annie pointed to the blank upper half of the wall. "I'm gonna draw a cloud town with cloud people."

"Your uncle doesn't care?"

"I don't even think he noticed," Annie said. "He hasn't come in my room since the day we moved in."

Natalie walked over to a small brown table opposite the bed.

"That's my homework desk," Annie said.

Natalie ran her fingers over the name "Jeremiah" carved in clumsy letters on the tabletop. "Who's Jeremiah?"

"Probably whoever had the table before me," Annie said. "Ralph got it at a garage sale for a dollar. Want to see my ring?" She reached for a wooden box on the table, and lifted the top.

"This was my mom's," Annie said, pulling a ring from the box and slipping it on her finger. "It's a ruby."

The ring had a gold-colored band and a red stone that bore the cloudy look of plastic. It reminded Natalie of the jewelry you get from vending machines outside the grocery store. The kind that turns your skin green.

"Very pretty," she said quietly.

"Thanks," Annie said. She centered the stone on her finger and admired her hand the way women in engagement ring commercials do. "It was my grandma's before my mom had it. What do they call that?"

"An heirloom?" Natalie said. It looked as much of an heirloom as the tab of a soda can. "Hey, I've been wanting to ask you something."

"Ask me anything, Olive. My life is an open book."

"How did your mom die?"

Annie gazed off into the distance. Natalie watched her eyes fill with tears.

"She had a really rare disease. It made her guts all sick and rotten, even though she looked perfect from the outside. She was really, really beautiful up until the day she died. But her organs turned to mush."

"That's awful," Natalie said. "What's the disease called?"

"It's so rare, there's not even a name for it," Annie said, twisting the plastic ring on her finger. "Maybe one day, they'll name it after my mom."

"That's really sad," Natalie said. "I'm sorry." She didn't know if she should believe the story, but she believed Annie's sadness. That was real.

"Thanks," Annie sighed. "Come wait by the window. Albert comes home right about now."

Natalie and Annie sat on the bed sipping lemonade and looking out the window at Albert's house. It was two-and-a-half stories tall with brown siding, and orange and yellow trim; the colors reminded

Natalie of autumn leaves. Most of the rooms didn't have more than one or two pieces of furniture. From where they were sitting, they could see down into Albert's foyer, which led into an enormous, nearly empty living room.

"Oop! Here he comes," Annie giggled.

Albert was coming up his front walk. His legs were so long that he seemed to take each step in slow motion, his endless arms swinging in time. An inky black ponytail rested on the collar of his light gray suit, and he wore polished, black shoes and carried a leather briefcase. Albert opened the door, ducking his head to avoid bumping the top of the doorframe. Calmly closing it behind himself, he turned the lock and set down his briefcase.

"Now watch this," Annie said.

Albert started jumping up and down in a frenzy. His shoes pounded the floor, his fists punched invisible enemies, and his face was pulled wide in a silent, furious scream. This all went on for about twenty seconds. Then, slowly, his energetic jumping and kicking turned into jogging in place. Soon, his legs and arms stopped altogether and he stood still. He let his head hang down for a moment and took a deep breath. Then, as if nothing strange had happened, he walked casually toward the back of his house and disappeared from view. Seconds later Albert reappeared in the kitchen. He opened the fridge, pulled out an apple, and took a big bite.

"What was *that* all about?" Natalie asked, her eyes still fixed on Albert. Annie shook her head.

"That's what he does every day when he comes home from work," she said. "I watch him a lot, since he's right next door. He's the most peaceful person, except for that."

"Is it because he lives alone?"

"I think he does it because he hates his job," Annie said. "In a few minutes, he's going to change into sweatpants and a T-shirt, and he might play some guitar. I think he hates wearing that suit all day and carrying that dumb briefcase."

Natalie nodded. "I would hate it, too."

Albert left the kitchen. The girls finished their lemonade, leaving sugary pink sand at the bottoms of the glasses. In a few minutes, they spotted Albert in an upstairs bedroom, now wearing a baggy pair of sweatpants, a white T-shirt, and white socks. He slid a long, black guitar case from under his bed. As he flipped the latches and lifted the lid, he smiled, as if seeing an old friend. Then he crossed his legs on the bed, settled the instrument in his lap, and started to play. The music put such a peaceful expression on Albert's face, Natalie wished she could hear it, too.

Chapter Eight

"Good morning, Mrs. Wallis. Is Natalie in?"

Natalie laid the book she was reading on the sofa and crept into the dining room. She hid behind the glass-sided hutch, and peered through the sparkly goblets and dishes into the foyer. Annie was standing on the hallway rug in her oversized choir robe, her dirty, bare feet sticking out at the bottom.

"Oh, you must be Annie!" Natalie's mom said. Her voice sounded strained.

"Indeed I am. It's such a pleasure to make your acquaintance at long last," Annie said, thrusting out a hand to shake. "I've been spending so many days

with your daughter, I felt it was high time that I introduced myself."

It was bizarre to hear Annie using such formal
words. Natalie breathed as quietly as she could, so
they wouldn't hear her. She didn't know why she was
hiding. She felt guilty doing it.

"Well, that's very thoughtful of you," her mom
said. There was a long pause, during which Natalie's
mom looked Annie up and down. "Did you come
straight from choir practice?"

"Dear me, no," Annie chortled. "I'm not in a
choir. I got this out of a box in the alley. Can you
believe someone was throwing it away? It's practically new."

Natalie's mom was wide-eyed and speechless.
"Maybe you girls would like some banana bread,"
she said finally. "It's homemade."

"That sounds delightful."

"Natalie!" her mom called up the stairs. "Sweetie?"
She disappeared into the living room and reappeared
in the dining room where, as she swept past the

hutch, she nearly ran into Natalie. "Oh, there you are. What are you doing back here?"

"I . . . I was getting a drink coaster," she said, stepping out from behind the hutch. Natalie waved hello to Annie, who beamed back at her.

"Let's sit and have some banana bread," her mom said. "And talk."

Before Natalie could protest, Annie slid into one of the dining room chairs.

"Wow, these don't look like they'd be comfortable, but they are," she said. "The fabric's pretty, too."

"Thank you," Natalie's mom said. "Sit, Natalie. I'll get the bread and some milk."

As her mom prepared the snack in the kitchen, Natalie took the chair next to Annie.

"What was with that formal introduction?" Natalie asked.

"I was trying to sound fancy, like the people on Charla's soap operas," Annie said. "Did I?"

"I don't know. I don't watch soap operas."

"That's right. You're a book reader," Annie said. She pointed at the hutch. "Is that stuff real crystal?"

"I'm not sure," Natalie said. "It could be."

"Did you know that if you pour grape juice into a real crystal goblet, it turns into wine immediately?" Annie asked. The word "wine" was followed by a stifled cough from the kitchen. Natalie held her breath. Annie's wild stories were okay when she and Annie were alone, but she didn't want her mom to hear any of them. If her mom already thought Annie was strange, hearing her lie would only make things worse.

At the casual sound of her mom slicing banana bread, the knife gently clacking against the china plate with each cut, Natalie exhaled. Maybe she hadn't heard after all.

Annie sniffed the air deeply. "Know what your house smells like?"

"No," Natalie said. "I can't smell it."

Annie closed her eyes. "It's a mixture of . . . cake and . . . something clean."

"Furniture polish," Natalie's mom said tartly, carrying in a tray of banana bread, two mugs of milk, and napkins. "Help yourselves," she said, setting the tray on the table.

Annie grabbed a large piece of bread — no napkin — and pressed it to her nose. "Yes, *this* is the good cake smell. Where did you buy it, again?"

"I didn't buy it anywhere," Natalie's mom said, taking the chair opposite Annie. "I baked it myself."

"You 'baked' it," Annie repeated to herself, mystified, as if the idea was completely foreign. Then she took a gigantic bite. Natalie reached for a small piece of bread and ate it carefully over a napkin.

Natalie's mom folded her hands under her chin and asked, "So, how are you settling in? You and your . . . uncle?"

Annie held up a polite finger until she swallowed.

"My uncle Ralph," she said. "We're good. Ralph likes it here because we're close to the bar."

"The *bar*?" Natalie's mom said.

"The Roundhouse Bar, where he works. He met Charla there."

"Charla?" Natalie's mom said.

"Ralph's girlfriend. You've probably seen her around. Long black hair, long red nails? She practically lives at our house."

"*Really*," Natalie's mom said, trying to share a horrified look with Natalie. Natalie let her eyes rest on her crumb-covered napkin instead. She wished she was down in the headquarters, or spying on someone, or riding her bike — anywhere but here, stuck in the middle of this awkward conversation between her mom and Annie. Why did her mom have to ask so many prying questions? Why did she have to examine Annie, as if she was a bug under a magnifying glass? Why did Annie have to answer in ways that confirmed the kind of girl Natalie's mom thought she was: repulsive and strange and rude? And for Pete's sake, would it kill Annie to wash her feet once in a while? Finally, Natalie couldn't stand it anymore.

"We have to go," she blurted.

"Oh?" her mom said. "Where are you going?"

"Just for a walk," Natalie said.

"Do you want a piece of bread for the road?"

"I'd love —" Annie began, but Natalie cut her off.

"We're full. But thanks anyway, Mom."

Natalie pulled on her cowboy boots and flew out the front door. She waited on the sidewalk as Annie shook her mom's hand good-bye and politely shut the screen door. When Annie reached the bottom step, Natalie asked, "Why did you want to meet my mom?"

"I don't know," Annie said, squinting into the sun. "You're really lucky to have a mom."

"I guess," Natalie said. She'd never really

thought that having a mom and a dad was lucky or unlucky. Just as she never thought about being lucky to have two arms and two legs. They were just there.

"Oh, I totally forgot!" Annie said. She pulled a white grocery bag from under her choir robe, and drew out several colorful plastic tubes. She handed three of them to Natalie and kept three for herself.

"What are these?" Natalie asked.

"Didn't you ever have a freeze pop before?"

"My mom makes Popsicles out of apple juice," Natalie said, shrugging. "She says they're healthier than the store-bought kind."

"Well, these are like Popsicles except there's no stick. We each get three flavors," Annie said, ripping open the top of one tube with her teeth.

Natalie held up a bright turquoise freeze pop. "What flavor is this?"

"Blue."

"Blue's not a flavor, Elvis. This looks like window cleaner."

"Trust me, it's delicious. I live off these things," Annie said. "Let's walk a little."

As they strolled down the block, Natalie tore into her red freeze pop first. She guessed it was cherry, and that seemed to be the safest to start with. She bit her front teeth into the ice and winced as pain shot through her forehead.

"Go like this, Olive." Annie demonstrated how to mash up the frozen part with pinched fingers, so the whole thing became slush. Then she blew into the tube to inflate it, tipped it upside down, and all the icy coolness slid down into her mouth. As the girls walked, Natalie blew into her plastic strip and tipped it upward. After the last drops of red slush had been emptied from the tube, Natalie sighed.

"These are good," she said.

"And they turn your tongue different colors. And they're cheap. And you can take them anywhere. In fact, I can't think of anything bad about them," Annie said. "Of course, I have to say that."

"Why?" Natalie asked. She pocketed the empty strip and started on her purple pop.

Annie took a modest pause. "Because my mom invented them."

Natalie examined the plastic package skeptically. "Your mom invented freeze pops?"

"Yep."

Natalie considered this as she blew into the tube and drained the slush into her mouth.

"Wait," she said after swallowing a chilly mouthful. "Wouldn't you be really rich now if she was the inventor?"

"Well, that's the thing. She had a soft spot in her heart for deaf people. After she made her fortune, she gave all the money from the freeze pops and the rights to the idea to a sign language association."

Lie, lie, lie, Natalie thought. "She donated *all* the money?"

"Yep. Every penny from the three million dollars she made with Franny's Freezies. And to say thanks, the association taught me and her sign language."

"So you know sign language?" Natalie asked.

"Yep. What, you don't believe me?" Annie narrowed her eyes.

"Oh, come on, Elvis," Natalie said. She waited for Annie to admit it was a joke, but Annie just glared at her. "I mean," Natalie continued, "you never said anything about it before."

"Because I'm not a bragger, Olive. That's why. Maybe you'd go around telling everyone something like that, but I wouldn't."

"Okay. Fine," Natalie said. "What's that called in sign language?" She pointed at a bird on a fence post.

Without a word, Annie made a gesture with both hands, one clenched in a fist and the other waving gently across her chest. It was complex and beautiful, like the sign language Natalie sometimes saw on the public-television channel. Annie's face was serene in the warm sunshine.

"That was pretty," Natalie said, trying to imitate the hand movements. "What does it mean?"

"Bluebird." Annie smiled.

"How do you say 'tree'?" Natalie asked. Annie brought both hands close to her face, palms open and facing out, and wiggled her fingers. Natalie mirrored the sign.

"Wow. That's so cool," Natalie said. "You should teach me more. Then we can do sign language when other people are around and we don't want them to know what we're saying."

"Smart idea," Annie said. "Look, this is the sign for 'secret.'" She clapped her hands twice without making any noise.

"Okay," Natalie said, mimicking the gesture. They continued walking, and soon passed in front of Steven Redding's house. Natalie dared herself to look. Noah was sitting on the porch swing, playing with action figures. No sign of Steven. She felt a mixture of disappointment and relief.

"Hey, Natalie!" Noah called out. "Wait a sec."

"What for?" Natalie asked. Noah *fip-fip-fip*ped over to them in his cardboard-stiff, midnight-blue jeans.

"I just wanted to say hi." He made his action figure wave with its little plastic hand.

"Okay. Hi." Natalie began pinching her last freeze pop to slush.

"What are you guys doing? Can I play?" he asked.

"We're not *playing*," Annie said. "Go back to your dolls." She did a complicated series of hand movements at Noah, ending with her two first fingers walking rigidly across her opposite palm. Natalie guessed it was sign language for "Noah's pants." She couldn't help laughing.

"What was that supposed to be?" Noah asked.

"It's sign language," Annie said.

"Yeah, right. You're just waving your hands around. Anyone could do that," Noah said. He tried his best to copy Annie, but all he could do was open and close his hands like lobster claws. Annie laughed.

"Who do you think you are?" Noah asked, pointing to Annie's robe. "It's not Halloween."

"The name's Annie Beckett. And if it's not Halloween, then why are you wearing that ugly mask?"

Noah touched his hand to his face, scowled, then stomped back to the porch swing.

"You people should be nice to me, you know!" he shouted. Annie and Natalie ignored him and kept walking.

"You wanna know the sign for my uncle's girlfriend?" Annie made an X with her two pointer fingers. "This means 'Charla.'"

"The deaf people made up a sign for your uncle's girlfriend?" Natalie asked.

"They have a sign for everything, Olive," Annie said.

"So what's the sign for 'Natalie Wallis'?"

Without a word, Annie made circles with the thumb and forefinger of each hand, and brought them up to her eyes.

"Are you making fun of my glasses?" Natalie asked.

"No. It's because you're a spy and you *see* things."

"Oh. Then what's your sign?"

"Oddly enough, Olive, it's the exact same as yours." Annie solemnly raised the circles to her eyes again. "And trust me, in sign language that doesn't happen very often. It's special."

Natalie wasn't sure she believed Annie. But she wanted to.

Chapter nine

"*One coffee with milk, please. Um café com leite, por favor.*"

"Oom cah-fay com lay-chee, por favor," repeated Mrs. Turner.

Mrs. Turner lived three houses down from Natalie, with a husband and a six-year-old daughter named Katy. She always made the best dessert for the annual block party, her flowers grew in neat rows, and she spent hours and hours weeding around each perfect plant. Mrs. Turner always waved to Natalie and said, "Hello, dear," when Natalie rode her bike past her house. She seemed like one of those moms on old-fashioned TV shows, the kind that was always smiling and had dinner ready at exactly six o'clock.

Mrs. Turner was sitting at a picnic table on her screened back porch, her dark brown face inclined toward a handheld tape recorder. Natalie and Annie were spying on her from inside the neatly trimmed hedge under the window. They heard the squeal of the tape rewinding, and watched Mrs. Turner screw up her face in concentration.

"One coffee with milk, please," the tape repeated. *"Um café com leite, por favor."*

"Oom cah-fay com lay-chee, por favor," Mrs. Turner said, this time with more enthusiasm. "Oom cah-fay com lay-chee, por favor!" She flourished one hand like an orchestra conductor.

"One ticket to crazy town, por favor," Annie whispered.

"She's learning a language from a different country," Natalie whispered back.

"A country that likes milky coffee, apparently."

"Shh. She'll hear us."

"*Where is the bathroom?*" asked the tape. "*Onde está o banheiro?*"

"Own-jay esta o bon-yer-oh?" Mrs. Turner asked back.

"*This completes lesson one,*" said a voice with a thick foreign accent. "*Please turn the tape to side two.*" Mrs. Turner pushed the stop button, then brought a stack of books from the picnic bench up to the table. Natalie squinted at the titles through the screen. *Brazil on a Budget. Your Guide to Rio de Janeiro. Brazilian Portuguese Grammar in Use.* Mrs. Turner opened *Brazil on a Budget,* and it flopped open to a page in the middle, as if it had been opened in the same place a hundred times. She rested her chin in her hand and stared at the page. Natalie wished she could see what Mrs. Turner was looking at. A pretty picture of the ocean? A description of her favorite town?

A low rumble in the street made the girls turn around. Mr. Turner was pulling into the driveway, his shiny blue car winking in the sun.

"Thank god for this hedge," Annie said. She tugged her robe to make sure the hem wasn't peeking out.

"No joke," Natalie said. She looked down at her bright pink cowboy boots, which she now considered her lucky spy shoes, and hoped they weren't showing through the leaves.

Mr. Turner shut off the engine and got out of his car. "Honey Bear," he called. "I'm home!"

Natalie and Annie swiveled back toward the porch to see what would happen next. Mrs. Turner grabbed the stack of books like they were on fire and she needed a place to douse them — quick. She decided on a little red wagon, which held her daughter Katy's dolls. As her husband climbed the back steps, she flung the dolls out of the way and spread the books on the bottom of the wagon. Then she tossed the bigger dolls back on top. She had just enough time to slip the tape recorder into her skirt pocket before the screen door opened.

"Hello, dear," she said, giving Mr. Turner a quick kiss. "How was your day? Would you like some iced tea?"

"That would be nice. With lemon?"

"Of course, dear. Let me fix it for you." Mrs. Turner opened the door to the house and they both went inside. Natalie and Annie snuck out from the hedge and walked swiftly down the driveway.

"Do they speak Portuguese in Brazil?" Natalie wondered as they reached the sidewalk.

"Yep," Annie said. "My mom spoke Portuguese fluently. She spent a year studying in Brazil." As Natalie looked at Annie for a long moment, her internal lie detector blared *baloney alert, baloney alert.* Annie kept staring straight ahead, down the block.

"Why do you think she's hiding her Portuguese lessons and travel books from her husband?" Natalie asked.

"Probably because when she runs away to Brazil," Annie said, "he's not invited to join her."

"Do you think Katy's invited?" Natalie asked.

"Nope. She's probably part of why Mrs. Turner wants to leave." Annie's voice sounded shaky, as if she might cry.

"Elvis, do you want to tell me something?" Natalie asked gently. Annie averted her eyes.

"No," she said defensively. "Why would I?"

"Never mind."

They walked in silence for a few paces.

"I bet she won't actually go," Natalie said at last. "She's probably just learning the language for fun."

"Secret fun," Annie said, brightening. She clapped her hands twice at Natalie without making any noise.

Natalie smiled. "That's another one for our headquarters."

Chapter Ten

It was near dusk on Saturday when Annie, wearing her choir robe, rang the Wallises' doorbell and asked Mr. Wallis if Natalie could come outside for a minute. Natalie sprang from the couch where her family was watching a show about African elephants. She put on her cowboy boots.

"Okay, but just for a minute," Natalie's dad said. "It's already getting dark."

"This won't take long, sir," Annie said, flashing her sweetest smile.

"What's going on?" Natalie asked once they were outside.

Annie flapped her arms in excitement, so her wide sleeves looked like bat wings.

"It's a surprise!" she said, swooping her face in close to Natalie's. "You're going to love it. Close your eyes."

Natalie squeezed her eyes shut, then snapped them open again.

"Wait, it isn't another dead animal, is it?" she asked.

"No, no. Just close your eyes and give me your hand." Natalie shut her eyes again and held out a cupped hand. Instead of putting something in it, Annie grabbed it and pulled Natalie across the lawn. "Now follow me."

"But I can't see anything," Natalie insisted, pulling back.

"Yeah. That's why I'm leading you," Annie said. "I'll tell you when you need to duck under a branch or step over a rock." Natalie stumbled blindly behind Annie, feeling the grass of her own yard become asphalt beneath her feet. She followed

Annie's instructions to hop over a crumbly piece of sidewalk and lean left to avoid a low tree branch. Suddenly Annie stopped walking and Natalie crashed into her.

"Oops," Natalie said. "Sorry, Elvis."

"No problem. Open your eyes. We're here."

It took Natalie a few seconds to understand where she was. They were standing in the alley next to a tall wooden fence, which Natalie recognized as Trina George's. The laughter of more than one person bubbled through the slats. Annie silently urged Natalie to look through the fence, the way you urge someone to open a birthday present you know they're going to love.

Natalie peered in and saw the source of the laughter. Two girls with long blond hair were sitting at the patio table, howling as if they'd just heard the funniest joke in the world. One of the girls was Trina, and the other was someone Natalie didn't recognize. On the tabletop between them sat two fast-food drink cups and several small, colorful bottles.

"Ashley, you first!" Trina cried, and pushed one of the cups toward her.

"This is gonna be gross," Ashley groaned. She removed the straw and plastic top, and cringed as she dipped her manicured hand into the cup. Trina nearly died laughing as her friend fished around the bottom of the cup. Ashley eventually withdrew her fist, coated in what looked like vanilla milk shake.

"*So* nasty," she giggled, dripping a puddle of shake on the table. When she opened her hand, something metallic clinked onto the glass tabletop. "But totally worth it. Look what I got." She pointed to the center of the milk-shake puddle.

"I can't tell what it is," Trina said. "You have to suck all the milk shake off." Ashley protested, but put the gooey object in her mouth. She swished it around for a few seconds, then slowly pulled a necklace from between her lips.

"Nice," Trina said, examining the pendant. "It's not real silver, though."

Natalie nudged Annie. "Did she steal that?"

"Yeah," Annie whispered back. "Before I came to get you, I heard them talking about how they do it. They walk around the store pretending to sip their milk shakes. Whenever they see something they want: splash — into the drink."

"That's shoplifting," Natalie said. "It's against the law."

"They walk right past the security guards. No one thinks to search the milk shakes."

"Is it really worth the trouble?" Natalie asked. "Whatever they steal gets all messy."

"It's so dumb," Annie agreed. "And see the perfume?" She pointed to the collection of bottles on the table. "They stole that, too. Hid it in their purses."

Natalie turned back to her gap in the fence in time to see Trina put the straw between her pretty pink lips and drink, until the last of the shake crackled at the bottom of the cup. Then, without soiling more than her fingertips, she pulled two small pieces out of the cup and popped them in her mouth like candy. After sucking them for a few moments, she spat a pair of earrings into her hand. From as far away as the fence, the gemstones sparkled.

"Are those diamonds?" Natalie whispered, and Ashley simultaneously screeched the same question.

"Shh!" Trina said. "They're pink sapphires. Fourteen-karat gold setting."

"Let me see!" Ashley demanded. She held the dazzling earrings in her palm and sighed longingly. "How did you do it?"

"The secret," Trina said, "is to ask the saleswoman to show you a bunch of earrings all at once. When they're on the counter, you pretend like you changed your mind and you want to see different ones. That gets her all mixed up, and then you act really annoyed at how stupid she is, and that makes her even more nervous. When you're sure she's totally confused, wait till she turns her back, then drop the pair you want into your shake." Trina held out her hand for the earrings.

Ashley reluctantly gave them back and asked, "How come you didn't get ones with diamonds?"

"The milk-shake method doesn't work with diamonds. They're so expensive, the lady will only show you one thing at a time. It's no good at fancy jewelry shops, either. They have too much security. You have to do it at a department store." To punctuate the end of her speech, she tapped Ashley's nose with a milk-shake-covered finger.

"Hey!" Ashley cried, wiping her nose. She then slurped milk shake up her straw and aimed it at Trina, spitball-style.

"Don't!" Trina pleaded, covering her face with her hands. "Please, Ash, this is a new shirt."

"So steal another one," Ashley said, then sputtered milk-shake dots all over Trina's shirt, hands, and hair. Without a word, Trina wiped away the drips and coolly selected a blue perfume bottle from the collection on the table. She flung the cap on the ground and grinned.

"Okay, sorry," Ashley said, backing onto the grass. "Sorrysorrysorrysorry!"

"Too late!" Trina cried, charging at Ashley. "Perfume war!" She pumped the nozzle as fast as she could.

"Oh, you're gonna get it now!" Ashley giggled. Pulling her shirt collar up over her nose, she sprinted through the fog of perfume to the patio table. She grabbed a green bottle and chucked the cap at the fence, where it nearly struck Annie in the eye. The frantic chase continued around the yard, both girls spraying and laughing hysterically until a heavy cloud of scent hung in the air. Natalie muffled a cough with her sleeve.

"Let's get out of here," she whispered, "before we suffocate. Or get blinded by flying perfume caps." Annie nodded and led the way back up the alley. When they were far enough from Trina's yard, Natalie said, "That was so weird."

"Yeah, I thought you'd like that," Annie said. "I know how much you love Trina."

"She makes me feel like screaming," Natalie said.

"So why don't you?"

"Because I'm not crazy?" Natalie suggested.

"Then I'll scream for you." Annie shut her eyes, threw her head back, and released the longest, most earsplitting scream Natalie had ever heard. Before she was done, the Turners' back porch light flipped on. A window on the other side of the alley lit up too.

"There. Feel better?" Annie asked.

"You're insane," Natalie said, pulling Annie's hand. "Let's go before anyone sees us."

When Natalie got back to her house, she was glad to find her parents and Ricky still watching the elephant show. They didn't seem to have heard Annie's scream. The loud stampede on TV probably covered it up.

Chapter Eleven

It was the middle of July already. The walls of the headquarters were covered with note cards, each telling a secret.

— *Sergeant Dewey is making a papier-mâché balloon.*

— *Albert Castle does a crazy dance when he comes home from work. He loves to play guitar.*

— *Mrs. Turner studies Portuguese and reads travel books about Brazil.*

— *Trina George and her friend shoplift jewelry using the Milk-Shake Method.*

— *Virginia Brooks eats face cream before bed.*

And lots more. There were so many note cards tacked to the walls, the room glowed white when the candle was lit. There was a secret about nearly everyone on the block. Except Steven, of course. Natalie was still working up the courage to spy on him.

"We're running out of room," Natalie noticed at the next meeting.

"We'll start sticking them to the ceiling," Annie said. "So, did you find any new secrets?"

Natalie told her about Clarissa Jackson, a young woman at the end of the block who prided herself on her beautiful flower garden.

"Her flowers are phony," Natalie explained as Annie took notes. "I saw her stick them into the ground really fast, like she didn't want anyone to see her doing it."

"I'm not surprised," Annie said, shaking her head. "I saw her pass off Chinese takeout as her own cooking last week. She dumped it out of the boxes onto her own dishes. Her guests thought she made it."

"Geez." Natalie plucked a green jelly bean from the pile on the blanket. "Anything else?"

"Well, after yesterday's meeting I was drinking a juice box in my backyard," Annie began. Natalie took notes in her neat handwriting. "I saw this chubby kid climb over Ms. Hatch's fence."

"Did he have a buzz haircut and a red face?" Natalie asked. Annie nodded. "That's Billy Frohman."

Billy was a twelve-year-old who lived two blocks away. He rode Natalie's school bus, but got on at the next stop. He was always making kindergarteners give up their seats for him and his duffel bag of hockey gear.

"He climbed into her yard from the alley. She has that high wooden fence, so I couldn't see him after he was in the yard. He was gone for a few minutes, and then I saw him coming over the side again, back into the alley. He was carrying a clay vase in one hand," Annie said.

"How did he climb back over without breaking the vase?" Natalie asked.

"He just held it in one hand and pulled himself over with the other arm and his legs." Annie leaned in close and whispered, "And that's the thing, Olive. Even though he's heavy, he was really fast about climbing back over. Like he's done it before."

"What do you think he does with all the pottery?" Natalie wondered.

"He sells it," Annie said matter-of-factly.

"He does?" Natalie asked, then crossed her arms over her chest. "Oh, you just made that up."

"You think I'm lying?" she said, getting up. "I'll prove it to you."

Natalie and Annie walked in silence for three and a half blocks. Natalie kept waiting for Annie to announce, "Here we are," but she didn't. Annie seemed lost in thought. The only sounds were the *slap-slap* of Annie's bare feet and the *clip-clip* of Natalie's cowboy boots.

Natalie became lost in thought, too. She thought about how Annie was brave about small things, like lighting matches and holding dead birds. And in some big ways, too, like screaming long and loud in the alley without worrying what anyone thought about her. But there was something sad about Annie that Natalie couldn't quite put her finger on.

"I know your parents don't like me," Annie said, breaking the silence. "But it's okay. I wouldn't want my kid to hang around someone like me either."

Natalie didn't know what to say. She wanted to insist that Annie was wrong, to comfort her. Only she wasn't sure Annie *was* wrong.

She was searching for the right words when Annie announced, "Here we are," and nodded to a yellow house on their left. "Billy sold them a vase."

"Really?" Natalie said, relieved to change the subject. "How do you know?"

"I followed him all the way from our street. When he got to the end of this block, he started ringing doorbells. The first couple of doors he tried, nobody was home."

"Didn't he see you?"

"No, 'cause I would hide a little ways back from him," Annie said. "When he rang the doorbell of that yellow house, I was behind the neighbor's pine tree. A man opened the door, and Billy took out a piece of paper and started reading it in this fake-nice voice. It said something like, 'Good afternoon, sir. I'm a member of the Westwood Boy Scouts, and today I'm selling handmade vases to raise money for the Blah Blah Something Something Homeless Shelter. Would you like to help us out today?'"

"Then what?" Natalie said, breathless.

"He unzipped his backpack and unrolled these white towels, and inside were the vases. He set five of them on the front steps, and the man chose one. The guy went inside and when he came out, he handed Billy — get this, Olive." Annie made an intricate gesture with her hands, which Natalie guessed was the sign for money.

"How much?" she asked.

"Ten whole dollars," Annie said. "He sold vases and pots to three other houses. One woman even bought two. He made sixty bucks in less than an hour."

"That's more than my dad makes per hour," Natalie said.

"Let's go through the alley," Annie proposed, pointing to the yellow house. "I'll show you the vase on their kitchen table."

When they got to the back of the house, Natalie peered in the window and spotted the vase. It was dressed up with a bouquet of dried flowers and was sitting on a lace doily, but Natalie recognized it as the same kind Ms. Hatch made.

Natalie turned to Annie and said, "You know, you're a really great spy."

"Thanks," Annie said, and made a gesture Natalie supposed was the sign for "thank you." "You're a great spy too. You just don't know it yet. And you're smart. And pretty. And nice."

Natalie felt her cheeks get hot and she had to bite her bottom lip to keep from smiling too wide. They were the nicest things anyone had ever said to her. And all at once. She looked down at her boots, bright pink against the dusty alley. *I'm smart. And pretty. And nice. And I'm a good spy,* she thought to herself.

As the girls walked down the sidewalk toward home, Natalie felt braver with each step. She kept hearing Annie's words echoing in her head — *you're a great spy, you just don't know it yet* — and they were giving her guts. *I never thought it was possible,* she thought, *but I'm ready to spy on Steven Redding.* She stomped her cowboy boots, as if smashing any remaining doubts.

"Whoa, Bigfoot," Annie said. "Keep it down."

"Oh. Sorry," Natalie said. "Hey, I need to spy on someone now. See you tomorrow?"

"Sounds good. I'm gonna see if Ms. Hatch needs help with her garden."

They agreed to have a meeting the next morning, then waved good-bye. Natalie scooted through a neighbor's yard into the alley. She passed the backs of five houses, and then she got to Steven's.

The rear of his red stuccoed house had a big wooden deck with a matching picnic table. The deck was elevated above the ground, and underneath there was a shaded area with sliding glass doors. Natalie guessed the doors led to a basement. Beside the doors rested a coiled garden hose and a stack of folding lawn chairs. There was something up on the picnic table, Natalie noticed, but she couldn't quite see what it was.

A car rolled slowly up the alley toward her, cracking a dried branch beneath its tires. When the driver looked at Natalie and smiled, she realized she was too visible. Natalie wedged herself between a pair of garbage cans and Steven's chain-link fence, which was covered in leafy vines. From her hiding spot, she had a closer view of the house, and anyone passing through the alley wouldn't be able to see her. She squinted at the picnic table, trying to decide what was on it. Action figures, she realized. Noah's.

Her attention was drawn down to the basement sliding doors. One of them glided open, and Natalie's heart raced. Steven stepped out into the shadow below the deck. He had gotten a haircut since she saw him last — a new, short style that made him even more adorable in Natalie's opinion. As he walked into the sunshine, he scratched his left cheek near the crescent-shaped scar she loved.

Steven began kicking the grass, at what seemed to be an imaginary soccer ball. He kicked the pretend ball harder now, as if going for the goal. He apparently made it into the net, because he pumped his fists in the air and mouthed the silent roar of the crowd. Steven smiled his irresistible smile at the imaginary stadium full of fans and waved. Natalie gave a tiny, slow wave back, so she wouldn't accidentally rustle the leaves.

A boy who was bigger and apparently older than Steven stepped out of the basement doors. His long blond hair told Natalie right away who he was: Tom Bechrach. He used to live in the house next to Annie's and go to Natalie's school. But his family moved across town last year and now he went to the junior high on the other side of the city. He was thirteen, and to Natalie he looked as big as an adult already. His chin even showed the wiry beginnings of a beard. Steven was friends with this guy? Juicy.

Tom had two younger brothers, and everyone knew the three boys as simply "the Bechrachs." All three of them were skinny, had long blond hair and green eyes. They were nine, eleven, and thirteen, and when they stood side by side in order of age, they looked like a milk commercial that shows how nicely a boy grows when he drinks three glasses a day.

The Bechrachs were always searching for easy ways to make money, and their methods had become neighborhood legend. Two summers ago, Tom, the oldest, came up with the idea for a barbershop. He dragged an old chair from their garage into the backyard, got a pair of scissors and a towel, and charged the neighbor kids twenty-five cents for five minutes in the chair and what he claimed would be a "high-fashion haircut." Gerry, who was nine at the time, was in charge of getting the kids on the block to stop riding their bikes or drawing with chalk and come get a haircut. John, the youngest, collected the money before they sat in the chair. The boys made seventy-five cents before Mrs. Turner came by, dragging her daughter Katy behind her. The pretty little girl was crying and tilting her head away so her brand-new bald patch wouldn't show.

Natalie was crouching by the fence, watching Tom and Steven kick the imaginary soccer ball back and forth, when she was startled by a loud *bang bang bang* behind her. She cringed as she turned toward the noise, thinking that someone had seen her and was calling her out. Natalie was not four feet from the noisemaker: a skinny, long-haired blond boy with green eyes. It was John Bechrach, banging a garbage-pail lid with a hammer.

"Keep it down, John!" Tom said. "Get in here." John entered the yard, and Tom yanked the lid and hammer out of his hands.

"Geez, I was just testing 'em out," John said.

"You're drawing a lot of attention, stupid," Tom said. "And if you had been listening to the plan, you'd know that's not what they're for."

"Okay, okay," said John. "Quit the lecture."

Natalie now saw Gerry Bechrach, the middle brother, coming up the alley. He was carrying a plastic pail of water and a yellow kitchen sponge.

"Ger," Tom called out to him. "Wait out there. We're ready to go."

"Are you sure about this?" Steven asked Tom, his eyebrows tilted with concern. Natalie melted.

"Are you kidding?" Tom asked. "It'll be awesome! Let's roll."

Natalie stayed behind the garbage cans until the group was halfway down the alley. When they were out of earshot, she crept out. Once the boys turned out of the alley, Natalie ran on tiptoe after them. She was careful to scurry behind a telephone pole or tree whenever someone in the group turned his head. *I can't believe I'm actually spying on Steven,* she thought.

She followed a safe distance behind as they walked toward the neighborhood's busiest street. The boys crossed and kept going straight until the next block, where they turned the corner.

Panicked that she might lose them, Natalie started running, stopping only to look both ways before she crossed the noisy, traffic-filled street. When she rounded the corner, she saw that the boys had stopped halfway down the block. She ducked behind a giant oak tree that smelled of dog poop, her heart pounding in her chest like the beat in a rock song. The Bechrachs and Steven stood in a circle fifteen feet away.

"Ger, you're in charge of position one," Tom spat out like a drill sergeant. "Tell me what position one entails."

"I go up to a car at the red light," Gerry recited, shifting from foot to foot. "And I start washing their windshield. I tell them that they can pay my brother, up there." He pointed at the next intersection of the busy street.

"Good," said Tom. "So just to review, you start washing the windshield of the car, even if they tell you to get lost. And then you say, 'You can pay that boy up there a dollar for our service.'" Tom then turned to his youngest brother: "And, Johnny Boy, you're position two. You stand at the next stoplight and do what?"

"I hold out the lid," John said, waving the dented trash can cover at Tom, "and I say, 'That'll be one dollar, and thanks for supporting our noble cause.'" John smiled widely and showed his missing front teeth.

"Wrong, stupid!" Tom shouted over the roar of a passing truck. "There's more to the speech, isn't there?"

"Oh yeah, I forgot," John said. "Then I say, 'If you don't pay, my brother at the next stoplight will dent your car with his hammer.' If they pay, I give you the thumbs-up. If they're a cheapskate, I go like this." He dragged his finger across his throat.

"Right. Good," said Tom. "So just to review, if John gives me the signal that someone didn't pay, I'm going to bang their hood with this hammer." He turned now to quiz Steven. "And Steve, what's your job?"

"Wait, I thought you said you weren't actually going to use the hammer," Steven said. "You said it was just for show."

"Hopefully that will be the case, my friend," Tom said, clapping Steven on the back. "Don't worry about it. Now let's review your job."

"I'm the lookout," Steven said, sounding anxious. "I make sure no cops are around. If I see one, I go like this." He waved both hands over his head.

Tom gave him a sharp nod of approval and commanded: "To your positions!"

Natalie watched the group split up and put their scheme into action. Gerry was the closest to her, holding his plastic bucket of water and kitchen sponge at the ready. Steven was a little farther down, nervously monitoring the traffic. On the next block was John, holding the aluminum lid out like a collection tray in church. And way down at the end of the second block was Tom. He was too far away for Natalie to make out his facial expression, but she could see him softly pounding the hammer into his palm, over and over, and she felt a nervous flutter in her stomach.

When two cars pulled up to the next light, Gerry did a sloppy job of washing their windshields. When he was done, each car drove toward John on the next block, stopping when they reached him. John gave his little speech about the hammer, and the first car clattered some coins into his lid. The second driver flicked a dollar at him. John gave Tom the thumbs-up for both cars, and Tom gave the thumbs-up back.

Their plan was working. At the next red light, there were three cars. Gerry washed the first two, and when he reached the shiny, red convertible that was third in line, he noticed that the light was about to turn green. In a hurry, he gave the driver his speech, but it was too late. The light changed. In a last-ditch attempt to make a buck before the driver accelerated, Gerry sloshed the entire contents of his water bucket across the windshield. The water rushed up and over the top of the glass and splashed the driver's face. After shouting a few swear words at Gerry, the driver squealed off down the street. The first two cars were pulled over by John to pay their dollars, but the guy in the third car zoomed right past. Natalie gasped. *That means that he didn't hear the part about the hammer,* she thought desperately.

John made a frantic throat-cutting gesture to Tom, who waved back in understanding. Natalie watched openmouthed as the convertible pulled up to Tom's red light. Tom calmly stepped into the street, raised the hammer high over his head, and brought it down on the hood with all his strength. Even though she was two blocks away, Natalie heard the nasty crunch of metal on metal. The driver screamed and flung open his door.

"Mission abort!" Tom whooped. Steven waved his hands wildly over his head, though no cops were in sight. Then the four boys scattered before the driver could get out of his car to chase them. And Natalie just stood there, staring down the block in disbelief. She felt as if she'd been hit by a hammer, too. Right in the center of her heart, where her crush on Steven Redding lived.

Chapter Twelve

That night, Natalie couldn't sleep. She lay awake thinking about Steven and what she had seen out on the street.

She turned onto her stomach and whispered to the paint-chip lady. *How could Steven be part of that awful plan? Will he be in trouble? What if the police catch him? Will he spend his life in prison? How will I marry him now?* The lady was a good listener, but she never gave any answers. That was the downside to a friend made of flaking paint.

It was raining the next morning, which fit Natalie's tired, gloomy mood perfectly. When she crawled into the headquarters for the meeting, she saw that Annie wasn't there yet. She was glad to sit for a minute alone in the dark, even if the air was a bit chilly. Natalie pulled her knees under her sweatshirt and hugged them. In the dim, moist silence, she imagined how a seed must feel, waiting deep in the dirt for spring. Anxious for what might happen next. She squeezed her eyes shut and saw the scene from yesterday. The red car. The hammer. The angry driver. And then came this terrible thought: *I have to tell Annie everything. I swore to share all my secrets with her.*

Swearing is serious business. Natalie read a book once where the main character broke a sworn promise to his friends. They got mad and pushed him off a horse, and the horse crushed his legs as it galloped away. In another book, a girl promised to wait for a prince in a castle tower, but she got tired of waiting and left. Lightning struck her as she fled. It just wasn't a good idea to break a promise.

"Ooh, it's wet," Annie said as she crawled through the hole. "This is when the worms come out."

"Yeah, I noticed," Natalie muttered.

Annie lit the candle. Natalie took a baggie of trail mix out of her pocket and tossed it onto the blanket. Aside from the smell of the rain, Natalie detected a strong flowery scent, like roses or jasmine tea.

Annie noticed Natalie wrinkling her nose.

"Do you like it?" Annie smiled. "It's my new pew-ferm." She sniffed her wrist deeply.

"Don't you mean *perfume*?" Natalie snapped.

"No, Miss Crabby, the label said pewferm," she said with conviction. "Because it stinks. I borrowed it from Charla."

"Stinks is right," Natalie said.

"So, what did you find out yesterday?" Annie asked. "You were so excited to spy on whoever it was."

Natalie anxiously grabbed a fresh note card and the pencil.

"No, you go first," she said. "I'll write."

"Okay." Annie took a raw peanut from the baggie and began roasting it above the candle flame. "Last night I was outside Mr. and Mrs. Warsaw's house.

I was looking in their den window, through the slit in the curtain — "

"Are you talking about that old married couple?" Natalie broke in.

"Yeah." Annie blew on the browned peanut and popped it in her mouth.

Natalie wiggled the tip of the pencil above the blank card and thought about the Warsaws. They were a little older than Ms. Hatch, and walked together up and down the block on sunny days, Mrs. Warsaw talking while Mr. Warsaw listened and patted her hand.

"Mrs. Warsaw was asleep in the reclining chair. Mr. Warsaw was on the other side of the room, sitting on the couch," Annie said. "He was hunched over the coffee table, which had a bunch of orange-and-white bottles on it. Know what those were, Olive?"

"Prescription drugs," Natalie said. "Duh, my dad's a pharmacist."

"Just testing you. So he was counting and sorting pills into little plastic trays. No big deal, right? I mean, they're old, they probably take lots of medications, but *then*," Annie said, and smiled mysteriously.

"Then *what*?" Natalie said, forgetting to be in a bad mood.

"Every time Mrs. Warsaw would shift in her sleep, Mr. Warsaw would cover his drug table real quick with a blanket from the couch. Until she went back to sleep, he'd stare at her like this." Annie imitated Mr. Warsaw's wide, frozen eyes and clenched jaw. "He was making notes in a notebook, too."

"Notes about what?" Natalie asked. Annie rolled her eyes.

"I'm Elvis, not Superman," she said. "I couldn't see that far. Anyway, there was a glass of milk on the table that I assumed was for him. But after he finished sorting the pills, he took an extra-large one and dropped it in the glass. Then he stirred the milk with the pencil he used to take notes."

"He stirred it with a pencil?" Natalie asked. She was writing so swiftly, her hand was in a cramp.

"Yeah, a dirty old pencil, then he woke Mrs. Warsaw and handed her the milk. She didn't want to drink it, but he stood over her till she finished the whole glass."

"Maybe he was just giving her medicine," Natalie said.

"Think, Olive. He hid the drugs every time she almost woke up. He stirred her drink with a pencil probably crawling with germs. Then he stood over her to make sure she drank it," Annie said, listing the reasons on her fingers. "Isn't it obvious? He's trying to *poison* her."

"What?!" Natalie scream-whispered. She couldn't write fast enough. "Are you sure?"

"I swear," Annie said, raising one hand. "I am not making this up. And the notes he was taking — I bet he was writing down the dose, to make sure he kills her slowly. Painfully."

"Whoa," Natalie said. Mr. Warsaw wasn't her friendliest neighbor, but he always listened so patiently to his wife on their afternoon walks. Maybe he finally got fed up of her nonstop talking, Natalie thought. "Should we call the police?"

"Not yet," Annie said, picking raisins out of the trail mix. "They would need solid evidence that he's poisoning her. She'd have to look half-dead, or be throwing up all the time. I'll keep an eye on her. If things get worse, we'll call the cops."

"Good plan," Natalie said. She reviewed her note card for spelling mistakes, chose a red pushpin, then tacked the card to the floorboards above. She looked around their headquarters. The walls were so completely covered in cards, the only empty spots were on the ceiling.

"Elvis, what are we going to do with all these secrets?" she asked.

"Leave 'em here," Annie said. She dumped the raisins she'd collected into her mouth. "Let some kid discover them fifty years from now. Just think. Someone will move into this house, start exploring, and find all these secrets."

"Our headquarters will be a time capsule," Natalie said. Annie looked confused, so Natalie added, "you know — something that preserves history for people in the future."

"Cool. Maybe we'll get famous," Annie said. "The future kid will find our time capsule, and they'll do a news story about it, and then someone will want to make a movie about us."

"And by that time, we'll be little old ladies knitting together, and we'll watch the movie, and we'll laugh because no one will know that we're Olive and Elvis."

"Exactly," Annie said. She picked a raisin from her back teeth. "But before we die, we'll write confessions and leave them next to our beds. 'I am Elvis.' 'I am Olive.' Then the world will weep because two of the greatest spies that ever lived are dead."

"Maybe they'll have a special funeral for us," Natalie said.

"They will. It'll be on TV. The schools will shut down for the day so everyone can watch. They'll give us each a huge marble statue on our grave, carved to look like us."

Natalie pulled her knees up under her sweatshirt again and imagined her grave statue. Would she be wearing her glasses? Her cowboy boots? Should she smile showing teeth or lips closed?

"Since we're going to be such big stars in the future," Annie said, "it makes me wish our secrets were a little more exciting."

"Yeah. Too bad a foreign secret agent doesn't live on our block," Natalie said.

"For all the future world knows, one does," Annie said, a crafty smile spreading across her face. "Who's going to deny it fifty years from now?" She pulled a card from the wall and read it aloud.

"'Sergeant Dewey is making a papier-mâché balloon in his basement.'"

Annie reached for a blank note card and the pencil. She copied the sentence onto the new card then pursed her lips in thought.

"'His army stuff is a cover-up for his real identity as a French secret agent. The balloon is like a satellite dish that picks up every classified conversation in the White House. If the president even sneezes, Sergeant Dewey hears it, and tells France.'"

"Ha! That's brilliant," Natalie said. "But hold on. Isn't it wrong to make up stuff and pass it off as true? I mean, these are real people."

"So?" Annie said, flicking the card with her thumb. "Nobody's going to see these. Not for fifty years at least. And anyway, it's just for fun." She plucked cards from the wall and handed a few to Natalie. "Here, help me fix these," she said.

For the next half hour, the girls sat in concentrated silence. They copied the existing secrets onto new note cards, and added juicy imaginary details.

"Listen to this, Elvis," Natalie said. "'Albert Castle loves to play guitar. But he has to work in a boring office instead of in a band, because his music is so beautiful, it would make the world stop turning if people heard it. And that would be bad for the environment.'"

"Yes! Now me," Annie said, clearing her throat. "'Trina George and her friend shoplift jewelry using the Milk-Shake Method. We have the pictures to prove it. Look for them in the next issue of *Teen Town* magazine.'"

"My turn," Natalie said, choking back a giggle. "'Billy Frohman steals Ms. Hatch's pottery and sells each piece for ten dollars,'" she read. "'Her pots and vases are crooked, but people still buy them. She is really a witch, and puts magic potions in all the pots she makes. Watch out, Billy!'" Natalie shut her eyes in a fit of laughter. When she opened them, Annie was staring at her harshly.

"No," Annie said, snatching Ms. Hatch's card away. "Don't make fun of her."

"Sorry," Natalie said, a little hurt. "I thought we were just having fun."

"We were," Annie said, her expression serious. "But we should get back to our real secrets now."

Natalie realized Annie meant her to tell about her spy mission the day before. She felt everything bad about yesterday come rushing back, carrying her away like rainwater down the gutter. She tried to muster the courage to tell the straight story about the car-wash disaster. But instead the story came out crooked, like one of Ms. Hatch's vases.

She told Annie about the Bechrachs and their plan to wash windshields, and how it all went wrong with the red convertible. But she only mentioned the three brothers — she never said anything about Steven Redding. When she was done, Annie whistled.

"Whew. I heard about that on the news last night," she said, then confusion spread across her face. "But wait, they said it was four boys, not three. Were there four?"

Natalie felt her stomach drop. "Yeah," she admitted. "There were four. The other one was . . . Billy Frohman."

"Well, that makes sense," Annie said. "He's an absolute criminal."

"Yeah," Natalie scoffed, happy to be off the hook. Annie reached for a blank note card and began copying down the secret. Without looking up, she asked, "So why did you say there were only three?"

"I dunno," Natalie said, trying to sound casual. "I guess I forgot that Billy was there."

"Ha!" Annie said. "You forgot he was there? More like you couldn't take your eyes off him. Why don't you just admit that you like him?"

"What?!" Natalie cried.

"Yeah, you have a crush on him," Annie said. "You went on a private spy mission just to see him."

"That's not true." Natalie squirmed. She wanted to prove Annie wrong, but couldn't see a way to do it without telling about Steven.

"It's totally true. Why else would you follow him? We've already got a huge secret on Billy, so there was no reason to follow him again," Annie said smugly.

"You're wrong," Natalie shot back.

"Look, all I know is that either you're madly in love with Billy, or you're such a lame spy that you had to follow the kid I already followed in order to get any sort of secret." Annie helped herself to another couple of raisins and sat back against the wall with an infuriating calmness. "Natalie and Billy, sittin' in a tree. Wow. Natalie Frohman — that will be your name, you realize. Wanna know the sign for Mrs. Frohman?" Annie puckered her lips and dramatically kissed each palm.

"Ha ha. That's hilarious, Elvis," Natalie said. She crawled toward the opening in the wall. "I think this meeting is over."

"See you tomorrow, Mrs. Frohman," Annie called out after her. "Maybe then you'll have a decent secret."

Chapter Thirteen

By dinnertime, Natalie was in a terrible mood. She was exhausted from her sleepless night. She was still worried about Steven. And the things Annie had said were gnawing at her. As her parents and Ricky chatted over their roasted chicken and parmesan risotto, Natalie ate her food in silence.

"I'm thinking about getting new curtains for the whole house," her mom said.

"That would be nice," her dad said. "Change the look of things a bit."

"I want spaceship curtains!" Ricky said. "Or pirate ships."

"Natalie, what kind of curtains would you like?" her mom asked.

"Whatever's on sale," Natalie said flatly.

"Pink, maybe?" her mom persisted. "I saw some cute pink ones with lace on the edges."

"Okay," Natalie replied. "Whatever."

"Hey, did you hear about those windshield washer vandals?" Natalie's dad asked. "It's hard to imagine those kids could be from our neighborhood. But that's what the authorities are saying. Ricky, more risotto?"

Ricky nodded and held out his plate. "What will happen if they catch the kids?" he asked. "Can kids go to jail?"

"I don't think so," Natalie's mom said. "But these days, who knows?"

"I'll build a jail for them. I'll lock them up!" Ricky cried.

"I bet you will," Natalie's dad laughed. "But you should just feel sorry for those kids. You have to have big-time problems to want to ruin someone's property like they did."

Natalie felt that hammer pound her heart again. *Is it true? Does Steven have big-time problems?*

"Can you believe these fireflies?" Natalie's dad said. "I never saw so many at once, not even when I was a kid."

Over the last week, thousands of fireflies had been lighting up the warm evenings like fallen stars. It was getting dusky outside now, and the fireflies were starting their nightly show. Natalie took a final bite of chicken and drained her glass of milk. She needed to be alone.

"I'm going to watch the fireflies," she announced.

As she pulled on her pink cowboy boots, her dad called out, "Don't wander too far, pardner." Natalie nodded and went out the front door.

She drew in a deep lungful of the evening air and stared across at Annie's house, which was dark except for a weak light in a second-story window. *Mrs. Frohman, Mrs. Frohman,* she replayed Annie's teasing. *Maybe tomorrow you'll have a decent secret.*

You'll see, Elvis, Natalie thought. *I'll get such a great secret, you won't be able to stand it.*

Natalie cut through her yard to the alley. As she walked, she kept telling herself to stop and peek in one of the houses. But her feet kept walking, almost against her will. Before she knew it, she was hiding between Steven Redding's chain-link fence and garbage cans, where she had hid the day before. *Okay,* she bargained with her feet. *I'll check in on him first, just to make sure he hasn't been dragged off to jail. Then I'll look for a secret that will knock Elvis flat.*

Natalie watched for activity inside Steven's house but saw none, so she focused on the fireflies lighting and fading in the air. She tried to follow one fly but it was impossible. Natalie would lock her eyes onto a brightly glowing point only to have it vanish into the darkness.

She imagined what Annie would think of this.

Geez, she'd say, *you can't even spy on a fly.* This lit something inside Natalie, but instead of a cool, green firefly glow it was a hot, angry flame that made her desperate to prove Annie wrong. Natalie crawled on all fours across the Reddings' back lawn, and looked up to where she knew Steven's room was. She stepped back and leaned on the chain-link fence for a better view into the second-story window.

The light was on, but she didn't see Steven. His ceiling was covered with glow-in-the-dark stars and moons. Two baseball pennants hung high on the wall. That was as much as she could see. She felt the unbearable prick of a mosquito on her shoulder and she brushed it away quietly, her eyes still fixed on Steven's window.

A head of black hair darted by, so fast that Natalie wondered if she'd actually seen it. Yes, there it was again. It was definitely Steven with his new haircut, and he seemed to be dancing. He bobbed close to the window now, and she could see he was wearing a large pair of headphones, the kind all the cool kids had. He nodded to a beat she couldn't hear, and scrunched up his face to the music. Natalie bopped her head, pretending that she and Steven were listening to the song together. Fireflies glowed around her, turning the summer night into a glittering disco. It was perfect. Absolutely, one hundred percent perfect —

"I see you down there, Natalie Wallis," came a harsh whisper. Natalie froze against the fence, her breath tight in her chest.

"Yeah," the voice said again, "I see you." She looked to the right of Steven's window, where the voice seemed to be coming from. There, framed by the white window was the shadowy outline of a person.

"Who is that?" Natalie croaked up at the window, her throat incredibly dry all of a sudden. She asked even though she knew.

"It's Noah," he said. "What are you doing?"

"Nothing," Natalie said a little too quickly. "I was following the fireflies, and there seem to be a lot in your yard. So I came closer."

"Wait there," Noah said. "I'm coming down."

Oh crud, Natalie thought. She considered running home, but Noah was already coming out the front door.

"Hi," Noah said, walking toward her. The light from his porch showed that he was wearing a too-small Disney World T-shirt, his indestructible blue jeans, and bare feet. "You look pretty," he said.

"Yeah, right," Natalie said, glancing down at her shredded cutoff shorts and plain T-shirt. "Well, I better go home." She headed for the sidewalk, longing to take one last look at Steven's window. But with Noah right there, she didn't dare.

"I know you were watching my brother," Noah whispered as she passed him, and Natalie stopped walking. "Both today and a couple of days ago. I saw you out in the alley. Do you like him or something?"

Natalie faced Noah and narrowed her eyes.

"I don't know what you're talking about," she said, with as much confidence as she could fake.

"I think you do," he said. "But I won't tell him if you stand out here with me for a minute."

"Why?"

"To watch the fireflies," he said. Natalie shoved her hands into her pockets, so hard that the white lining peeked past the frayed hems.

"Fine."

"And you have to hold my hand." His shifty eyes glimmered.

"What?" she hissed. "No way."

"Or I can just tell Steven right now," he said.

"This is ridiculous," Natalie said. She set her jaw and offered her limp left hand to Noah. She might have to amputate it when this was over.

"Let's look at the ones over here," Noah said, leading her into his front yard. "You going to the block party on Saturday?"

"Yes," Natalie said. She wasn't going to say anything more than she had to.

"We're bringing chicken wings," Noah said.

"Yum."

Noah stepped onto the sidewalk and pointed to a cluster of lights. Natalie drew her shoulders up to her ears, as if this could hide her from anyone who might be watching.

"Ooh, look at that one," he said, pointing his toe at a firefly landing on the concrete. It turned its light on and off quicker than usual, as if putting on a special show for them. Natalie leaned in to inspect it, close enough see its tiny antennae twitching. It glowed incredibly bright, the neon yellow-green peeking through the insect's dark wings. It was beautiful.

Suddenly, Noah slapped his bare foot over the fly, scraping it dead across the concrete. For a couple of seconds, they watched the bright green streak fade to a sad black. Natalie blinked in disbelief.

"You killed it," she whispered. She flung his hand away from hers. Her face and throat got hot and she felt sick to her stomach. She turned to Noah and shoved him back onto the grass. "YOU KILLED IT!" she shouted.

Noah regained his footing and crossed his arms over the faded Mickey Mouse on his chest. "Big whoop. It was a bug," he said.

Natalie crouched carefully over the black streak, which didn't even look like a bug anymore. It could've been a scratch made with a burnt stick, or a scuff from the sole of a boot.

"I can't believe you did that," she said.

"Sheesh. Why don't you have a funeral or something." Noah waited for her to say something back, but Natalie just kept staring at the sooty mark. After half a minute of silence he said, "I'm going back in. And I might still tell Steven that you were staring at him."

"Do whatever you want, you jerk," Natalie said.

"Fine. But you'll be sor-ry," he said in a sing-song voice.

Natalie remained hunched over the black smear. She listened to Noah *fip-fip-fip* back to his house and slam the screen door. When he was gone, Natalie stood up. She felt her anger fade like the firefly had, leaving behind a sadness that made her eyes water.

Everything was wrong. Natalie was a bad spy. Noah caught her in the act, and on her most important mission — spying on Steven. Now Noah would probably tell his brother that she was watching his window, and Steven would think she was a creepy weirdo. But who was she kidding? Steven would never like her back in a million years anyway.

Natalie's feet began walking on their own again. She thought about what she'd tell Annie the next day. Would she admit that Noah had caught her? She got caught, and she didn't even have a good secret to share. So lame.

She walked down a few blocks and back up again, lost in thought. A loud clatter came from an upstairs window. When Natalie looked toward the noise, she realized she was standing in the alley behind Annie's house. A pair of skinny arms slammed open the shutters of the upstairs window, and Natalie quickly pressed her back against the shadowy side of Annie's garage. The streetlamp illuminated Charla and her long, shiny black hair. She climbed out the window onto the balcony one high heel at a time, struggling to keep her balance with a cordless phone in one hand and a pack of cigarettes in the other.

"Hi, Terrence. Is my sister there?" Charla said after dialing. While she waited, she tweezed a cigarette from the pack with her long fingernails and lit it. She sipped the tip, then blew a smoky stream from the side of her mouth. "Hey, girl, how are you? . . . good, good. Yeah, I'm at Ralph's. He ran to the grocery store but he'll be back soon. Hold on . . ." Charla looked back at Annie's bedroom window. It was dark.

"Good, no one's here," she told her sister. "So Ralph's bratty niece used my perfume *again*. That stuff isn't cheap, you know. And she goes digging through my purse. She tells every kind of lie under the freakin' sun. But I'm supposed to be nice to her because she's had a rough year." She puffed on her cigarette angrily. "Rough year? I've had a rough *life*."

Charla listened to her sister for a minute, nodding. Then she said, "I don't see why Ralph has to be her guardian. But he keeps saying, 'She's family' like that means everything. It's a crummy reason if you ask me. But apparently there's no one else to take care of her."

For a second, Natalie thought she saw something move in the darkness of Annie's window. Maybe she imagined it.

"Didn't I tell you?" Charla continued, "Ralph's sister — the little brat's mom — left her at Ralph's house in Resselville a year ago. She went out and never came back. Not even the police could find her." Charla stared blankly at her shrinking cigarette, her bright red mouth half-open as she listened to her sister talk.

Natalie's jaw hung slack too, but in shock. *Her mom went out and never came back?*

"The little sneak tells anyone who will listen that her mom is dead, but it's a lie. That lady is probably whoopin' it up at some casino in Las Vegas, while I'm stuck here dealing with her kid." Charla flicked the cigarette butt down into the yard and walked back to Ralph's window. She sat on the sill.

"Don't get me wrong. Ralph's been a saint to this girl, and that's real nice of him. But I wish it could just be me and him. I mean, if we get married, what's Annie gonna be? I ain't never heard of a step-niece."

Charla then got into a heated debate with her sister about what color her wedding gown should be — purple or yellow — and whether she should wear a veil or not. Natalie pushed away from the garage wall as quietly as possible and tiptoed back up the alley. She turned the new secret over and over in her mind like a penny you find on the street.

Her mom's not dead, she ran away. Her mom's not dead, she ran away.

Natalie had wanted to be a great spy. To witness a fantastic, terrible secret without anyone seeing her.

She wanted to discover something that would shut Annie up. And unfortunately, she had.

In bed that night, Natalie felt angry and confused and sad all at the same time. She stared at the ceiling fan above her bed, at the blades cutting swift circles through the air. *Whoosh, whoosh.* Her thoughts went round and round too, and she couldn't sleep.

She always knew that Annie was a liar, and she never liked it. But she thought Annie's lies were just little exaggerations. Annoying, yes, but as small and harmless as mosquitoes. But this new lie was not small or harmless. Annie pretending that her mom was dead when she wasn't — it was the queen bee of lies. And Natalie had been stung. She fell for it. She felt angry and betrayed, like the whole time they had been friends was poisoned now. Did Annie think Natalie was stupid? Was this her idea of a joke? Natalie was so sick of trying to guess all the time if Annie was telling a lie, the truth, or a combination of both.

She was also confused. Why would Annie want to lie about her mom being dead? Normal people don't kid about that kind of thing. If you're trying to trick a friend you say something like "Hey, your fly's open" or "Look, there's a ten-dollar bill on the sidewalk." You don't say, "My mom's dead," unless it's really true. Dead parents just aren't joke material.

Natalie was sad, too. Sad because Charla was awful to Annie. Sad because Annie's mom went out and never came back. And sad that Annie never trusted her with the truth.

Angry. Confused. Sad. *Whoosh, whoosh.* Her feelings followed the fan blades around and around.

Natalie longed to share this secret with someone who wouldn't ever tell, like a dog or a hamster. She didn't have a dog or a hamster. The best she had was that face made of chipped paint on the headboard of her bed. Under the *whoosh* of the fan Natalie told the paint-chip lady about everything: Annie's big secret, Annie's lies, her crush on Steven, and even the firefly Noah killed. Then angry, confused, sad, and exhausted, she fell asleep.

Maybe she made the decision in a dream, or maybe the paint-chip lady whispered the answer to her while she slept, because when she woke up the next morning, Natalie had resolved to get everything out in the open with Annie. She'd tell her what she'd heard in the alley. Natalie would clean her insides of every last burning secret, right down to her crush on Steven. Tell the whole truth and nothing but — that's what friends should do, right? And that's what a good spy is after: the truth. She'd find out why Annie had lied about her mom, too. And Natalie would do all this before the block party at noon.

There. It was decided.

Chapter Fourteen

"Elvis, I have to talk to you. Right now." Natalie stood on Annie's front stoop. "Meeting?"

"Sure," Annie said.

As they walked around to their headquarters, the girls saw people setting up tables in the middle of the street for the block party. The orange-and-white blockades were up on both ends of the street, so no cars could come through. Their neighbors, all the people they'd spied on, were locking their front doors and carrying casserole dishes and plates of cookies into the street. Natalie saw her mom and dad putting a checkered cloth on a folding table. Close by, Ricky was setting up his crooked wooden carnival rides.

They were sitting in the headquarters, the candle lit. Annie tossed two Ho Hos cake packages onto the blanket.

"Okay, Olive," she said. "Shoot."

The way Annie was looking at her, so intently, Natalie felt that the secrets must be showing right on her face. She had better get them out quick. But first she'd have a Ho Ho, for courage. Natalie tore open the wrapper and took a huge bite of the cake. Annie opened hers too and started sucking out the cream.

"All right," Natalie began, her throat thick with frosting, "I'm gonna start with the easier secret." She took a deep breath. "You know how I told you about those boys that did that window-wash thing? I wasn't completely honest about that."

"I knew it," Annie said. "You lied. Miss Honest lied to me."

Natalie dropped her gaze to her lap. "Elvis, I'm sorry I lied. But it was because I was embarrassed."

"Embarrassed? Why?"

"Because the other boy was Steven Redding." Natalie felt her face flush hot as she said his name.

"Is that the boy with really black hair? Wow, he doesn't look the type to commit crimes. So what about him?" Annie demanded.

"I like him." Natalie shrugged. "Maybe I love him." There was a silence in which Natalie couldn't bear to look up. Then Annie spoke.

"Oh. My. God." She threw the rest of her Ho Ho down on the blanket and grabbed Natalie by the shoulders. Natalie braced herself for Annie to do something crazy, like spit in her face. Or body-slam her against the wall.

Instead, she gave Natalie's shoulders an excited little shake and said in a fiery whisper, "You're in *love*. Don't you know that this is what life is all about? This is what people all over the world dream of their whole lives and now you have it. In soap operas, people faint when they're in love. Do you feel like fainting? Oh, Olive, you are so lucky."

This was not the reaction Natalie was expecting. She didn't know what the reaction would be, but certainly not this. Annie spat on the candle, then grabbed Natalie's hand and tugged her firmly toward the opening in the wall. Natalie's news seemed to give Annie a superhuman strength way beyond her tiny body.

"Come on," Annie said with great determination. "We have something important to do."

"What?" Natalie asked, completely confused. Annie was pulling her hand so hard, Natalie had no choice but to follow. "Hey, I didn't finish my Ho Ho," she said.

"Who cares?" Annie said, towing her out into the sunlight. "Who cares about cake when we're talking about love?"

The bright daylight made Natalie squint, and she stumbled blindly behind Annie's astounding grip.

"This is going to be amazing," Annie muttered under her breath.

"Where are we going?" Natalie asked.

"You'll see, you'll see," Annie sang gaily. They were in the street now, rushing toward the cluster of people and folding tables in the middle of the block. They were close enough to the party that the aroma of chicken wings and hot dogs wafted over them. They passed Ricky's carnival: the splintery slide, a lopsided mini Ferris wheel, and an unidentifiable mishmash of pine boards.

"I see him! Steven!" Annie called out. Natalie's stomach dropped. She watched in horror as a dark-haired figure turned his head toward them.

"Me?" he said, and began walking over.

"Let go!" Natalie said, frantically tugging away from Annie's iron grip. Annie released her hand in surprise.

"What's wrong?" Annie asked.

But there was no time for an answer, because Steven was standing right next to them.

"Were you talking to *me*?" he asked.

"Yes. Hi," Annie said, and grinned. "I'm Annie. And this —" she pushed Natalie in front of Steven, "is Natalie Wallis." Natalie lowered her eyes to Steven's tennis shoes.

"Yeah," Steven said, obviously confused. "I know her. She rides my bus." Natalie's heart wasn't just beating fast. It was giving fitful little jumps as if preparing to make a break for it out of her chest. "Are you okay?" he asked, craning his neck to see Natalie's face, which was burning with shame. All she could do was nod and take a deep, shaky breath.

"You're probably wondering why we called you over here," Annie said with mounting excitement. "Well, it's because —"

"Shut up, Annie," Natalie said viciously.

"All right," she said, nudging Natalie toward Steven. "*You* tell him then."

"Tell me what?" Steven asked gently. Natalie swallowed back tears and prepared to speak, but Steven spoke first.

"Is it that you like Noah? I already know. He said that you guys are boyfriend-girlfriend now."

Noah strolled up behind Steven, eating a chicken wing.

"That's not true!" Natalie cried. Her glasses began to fog.

"It's not?" Steven asked. "Noah said that last night you guys were hanging out in our yard. He told me about how you held hands and kissed." Steven looked back at Noah, and Noah nodded.

"That is such a lie!" Natalie shouted, her breathing jagged. "I would never kiss him! He forced me to stand with him and hold his hand."

"She likes you, actually," Annie piped up.

"Shut your fat mouth, Annie," Natalie growled.

"Whoa, what?" Steven said.

"And she saw you smashing car hoods with the

Bechrachs the other day," Annie said, "but she didn't tell anyone because she's in love with you. She just confessed to me."

"Oooookay," Steven said. By now, Noah had stopped eating the chicken wing and just stood there, staring.

Natalie had never felt so ugly in her whole life, standing with a flame-red face and foggy glasses in front of her favorite boy. This was not how Steven was supposed to see her. In that terrible moment Natalie found her own superhuman strength. She grabbed Annie's shoulders in a death grip.

"How dare you?" she shouted, shaking Annie. Everyone at the block party turned to look, but that didn't stop her. "You want to embarrass *me*? I'm going to embarrass *you* so bad you'll wish you were never born!" The street was silent except for Natalie's voice. "That's right. I know a secret about you."

"You do not," Annie challenged. She tried to steel her face, but there was fear behind her eyes.

"I know that your mom isn't dead. She just ran away."

"That's a lie," Annie said, her voice shaky.

"Yeah, right!" Natalie let loose a crazy laugh. "I heard Charla telling her sister on the phone last night. I heard everything." She felt completely out of control now. Her anger was like a runaway train, speeding to an inevitable crash.

"You know what else I think? Your mom didn't invent freeze pops. And that sign language you do? It's totally fake. And you were never in any movie, either. Everything you ever told me was a BIG FAT LIE."

Annie's face was emotionless, except for two straight tear lines tracking down her cheeks. Though Natalie's back was to the party, she could feel everyone staring. Steven, her parents, all the neighbors. None of that mattered now.

"You are the meanest person I've ever met," Annie said with quiet rage, "and I'm never talking to you again. I hate you." She ran toward her house, and didn't stop until she had slammed the screen door shut.

Natalie couldn't bear to turn around and face the party. Maybe Steven was still standing two feet behind her. Or maybe he had wanted to get away from her, and jogged back to the group. She didn't know. Maybe everyone else on the block, including her family, was still staring at her, this insanely mean girl who just tore her friend into a million pieces. But Natalie didn't turn around to check, so she didn't know. She just ran straight home.

Chapter Fifteen

Natalie quickened her pace as she felt the tears coming. She dashed up the front steps to her house, and extended her hand for the doorknob long before it was within reach.

There was a loud *fip-fip-fip* behind her.

"Natalie," Noah said, breathless from running to catch up.

"What do you want, you jerk?" Natalie asked.

"Just to let you know that you can still be my girlfriend."

"Excuse me?" Natalie said.

"Yeah, I'll take you back," Noah said, moving closer. "You know, since it's not going to work out with Steven." He placed a clammy hand on her shoulder and gave her a condescending squint. "He's really too old for you."

Natalie shrugged his touch away. "I'd *never* be your girlfriend. You stupid coward bug murderer." She watched her words cut him like tiny knives.

"You're gonna be real sorry you said that to me," he said, his voice wobbly with tears.

Natalie saw her parents coming toward her, Ricky running behind them. She jerked open the front door and flew up the stairs. Once in her bedroom, she locked the door, tore off her glasses, and collapsed facedown on her bed, the tightness in her chest dissolving into loud, aching sobs. She couldn't remember a time when she'd felt so awful.

"Natalie?" she heard her mom call up the stairs. "What's going on?" Her mom rattled the doorknob. "Natalie. Let me in."

"No."

"What's all this about?" Her dad's voice came through the door. "What were you and Annie fighting about?"

"Nat, are you sad?" Ricky asked.

"Just please go away," Natalie cried. "I need to be alone."

There was silence outside the door for a few moments, then Natalie heard them walk away. She buried her face in her pillow again.

I hate Noah, she mouthed. *And I hate Annie. I hate herIhateherIhateherhatehersomuch.*

She lifted her head and looked at the paint-chip lady. Instead of appearing to wait for Natalie to tell her a secret as usual, her head seemed to be turning away. As if she couldn't bear to look at Natalie.

I hate everyone, she whispered to the tiny silhouette. *Even you.*

She cried until her ribs felt sore from so many sharp, angry breaths. When she couldn't cry anymore, she dropped into a deep sleep.

✳   ✳   ✳

When Natalie woke up, it was nighttime. She put on her glasses, shoved her feet into her cowboy boots, and ran downstairs, whipping past her parents and Ricky, who were playing a board game in the living room. Her parents called after her, but she was already outside, wheeling her bike from where it rested against the house. She took off — no helmet — down the block.

It was dark and Natalie couldn't see any of the sidewalk cracks, but she knew them by heart and swerved around each one. Her anger pushed her to new limits of speed. She careened around the familiar corners, pumping the pedals hard, her leg muscles on fire. When she got to the foot of the big hill, Natalie bore down on the handlebars and concentrated on the work. She didn't think about what she'd said to Annie. She didn't feel humiliated about her crush on Steven. She didn't worry about Noah's threat. For the first time since the fight that afternoon,

Natalie felt free. And then, without warning, she crashed into something in the dark.

"Whoa!" a voice cried out. Natalie heard the dull thud of someone hitting the ground, followed by a wincing "Ooh. Ow."

She recognized the voice. It was Steven.

"Oh, no." Natalie cringed. She jumped off her bike and threw it on the grass. "Are you okay?" she asked, kneeling beside him. "I'm so sorry."

"It's no big deal," Steven said, inspecting his skinned elbow. "Can you just help me up?" He reached his hand out without looking at her. Natalie grabbed it and felt a warm electric tingle climb her arm. As she pulled Steven from the ground, a look of recognition came across his face.

"Oh, Natalie," he said. He said it the way you might say, "Oh, free ice cream" or "Oh, all-day recess."

"You know my name?" she asked.

Steven laughed. "Of course I know your name. Your friend introduced us today. And we have the same bus stop."

"But I've never heard you say it before," Natalie said.

Steven gave her his adorably crooked smile. "Well, I never heard you say my name, either."

"Because I'm SHY," Natalie said, louder than she meant to. "I mean, I'm shy," she repeated in a whisper.

"So am I," he said, flashing that magic smile again. "But two shy people can be friends, can't they?"

"Of course," Natalie said. Her heart grew so warm, she felt like she had swallowed the sun. She imagined that if someone was watching from a few blocks away, she would be glowing and twinkling like a distant star.

"But *just* friends, okay?" Steven asked.

Natalie's glow dimmed, her star collapsing in on itself. "Just friends," she said with a firm nod, hoping she didn't sound sad. "So, why are you out here this late?"

Steven's face grew serious. "I was thinking about that thing with Tom Bechrach — walking and thinking. I didn't know he was actually going to use the hammer. I feel so bad about it. I told my parents the whole story already."

"You told them?" Natalie asked.

"Yesterday. Then my mom called Mrs. Bechrach, and Tom probably won't ever talk to me again," he said, kicking a weed from a crack in the sidewalk. "But I don't care. He's a jerk anyway."

"Wow," Natalie said. "I can't believe you told your parents."

"I had to. I felt like such a bad person."

When he said this, Natalie remembered everything her bike ride had helped her forget.

"You're not a bad person," she said, and hurried over to her bike. "But I am."

"I doubt that," Steven said.

"It's true," she said. "You saw my fight with Annie. She said I'm the meanest person alive, and she's right." Natalie mounted her bike and as she pushed away, gave him a hopeless little wave good-bye.

Chapter Sixteen

The next morning, Natalie came down late to breakfast, her head aching from all the crying. Her parents looked at her with wide, almost frightened eyes, as if she had grown a third ear during the night.

"Where did you run off to last night?" her mom asked. "We were worried."

"I rode around the block," Natalie said, pouring herself a bowl of cereal.

"At night?"

"I had to think about some stuff, okay?" Natalie said.

"No, Natalie Marie, it is not okay to ride your bike at night," her dad said.

Natalie rested her head in one hand. It felt so heavy.

"Is this about Annie? Or that boy Steven?" her mom asked.

"It's complicated," Natalie sighed. Before she could explain further, she saw something *whoosh* in through the mail slot. There on the entryway rug lay three white note cards.

"Mail on Sunday?" Natalie's mom said, picking up the cards. "'Ricky Wallis throws used tissues behind his bed. He's saving them to sew a parachute one day,'" she read from one. "'Discovered by Elvis and Olive, June 10th.' What is this?"

No, Natalie thought. *Please, no.* She rushed to the living room window and looked out. Across the street, someone was reaching for the mail slot in Ms. Hatch's door. Noah. He must've stolen the cards from their headquarters. Natalie knew he wanted to get back at her, but she never imagined he'd do something like this. She had no idea he knew the headquarters even existed. Natalie felt like she might throw up.

"There's something on the back," Natalie's dad noticed from where he sat. Her mom flipped the card over and read the boyish scrawl.

"'Elvis is Annie Beckett and Olive is Natalie Wallis,'" she read. She turned to her daughter. "Natalie, what is the meaning of this?" Natalie didn't answer. She just pulled on her cowboy boots.

"If you leave before you explain yourself, you're grounded," her mom said.

Natalie didn't say another word. She simply ran out the door.

Natalie sprinted across the street to Noah, who was coming down Ms. Hatch's front walk. Maybe he hadn't given secret cards to all the houses yet. If not, she was going to stop him.

"You're gonna get it!" Natalie yelled. When

Noah saw her, he started running down the block toward his house. Natalie dashed after him. Even though he was wearing his stiff jeans, his tennis shoes gave him an advantage over Natalie's cowboy boots. He darted across the street to his house, where Steven was dribbling a soccer ball in the front yard. Steven collared Noah.

"Whoa, man," Steven said. "What's up?"

Natalie caught up to them.

"I was just making a few deliveries," Noah said, glaring at Natalie. "I'm all done, though." Natalie tried to swallow the huge lump forming in her throat. *Oh no*, she thought. *There's no hope.*

Nearly the whole neighborhood was built by the same construction company around eighty years ago, so there were many things about the houses that were similar. Each had a garage in back. Each had a little crawl space under the porch. And each had the kind of mail slot that drops letters right into the porch or front hallway. Unlike a mailbox that hangs on the outside of a house, this type of mail slot doesn't let you reach in and get a letter back. So there was no way to retrieve the cards Noah had delivered.

Steven sent Natalie a questioning look, then gave Noah a shake.

"You better tell me right now what's up," Steven warned.

"Don't you know?" Noah laughed. "Natalie's a spy. She's been spying on the whole neighborhood and writing down people's secrets. Her and that new girl, Annie. All I was doing is telling people what they deserve to know."

Steven looked from Noah to Natalie, as if trying to decide if this was for real. Natalie cut the suspense.

"It's true," she told him. "I'm as awful as you think." And for the second day in a row, Natalie ran away from Steven.

As she dashed up the hill toward her house, she felt totally alone. She couldn't go back home, because her parents would be waiting for an explanation and without a doubt, she'd be grounded. She couldn't stay out here, where all the neighbors might see her. She imagined them, an angry mob chasing her down the street, shaking their note cards at her. She couldn't go to Annie, who had said she hated Natalie and never wanted to speak to her again. She needed a place to hide and gather her thoughts. Natalie picked the only good hiding place she knew.

She scanned the front of Annie's house for signs of movement, but saw none. She checked behind her, where Steven and Noah had been, and saw they had gone either around back or inside. The coast was clear. Natalie ran across the street and crawled through the hole under Annie's porch.

She felt along the ground and found the candle stub, which hardly had any wick left. Annie was always the one to light it, but Natalie would have to do it herself this time. She lit the candle before the match flame could creep too close to her fingers. In the orange glow, Natalie gazed around the little room. Every last note card had been ripped from the walls and ceiling, leaving a treacherous layer of pushpins on the dirt floor. She brushed them away from her usual spot against the wall and sat down.

Before the block party, Natalie hadn't known how it felt to have a treasured secret exposed. But after standing in the middle of the street, where her crush was broadcast in front of Steven and everyone, she understood. It was like a nightmare, the kind that makes your heart pound whenever you remember it. That's just how she and Annie made all the neighbors feel with their spying game. Or maybe they felt even worse, because the true secrets were mixed with false ones. What a horrible mess. And as much as she wanted to, Natalie couldn't blame Noah completely.

No, she thought. *Annie and I started this. It's all our fault.*

In fairy tales, when people do bad things, they're banished from the kingdom. Paint an ugly portrait of the king? You're banished. Laugh at the queen's new hairdo? Banished. If you steal a loaf of bread at the marketplace — leave, and don't ever come back. Surely, Natalie thought, spying on your fellow villagers was a banishable offense. She had stolen everyone's privacy, and she couldn't give it back, like a loaf of bread. There was no way to undo any of it. Would they send her away?

At that moment, the candle burned out, and Natalie was left in the dark. She felt her way over to the crate in the corner and lit a match to see inside. Underneath a few bags of junk food, she found an unused white candle. She also discovered something else: her old notebook from school, the one she'd let Annie keep on that first day of summer. She lit the new candle and opened the notebook across her knees.

In the flickering light, Natalie thumbed through the pages. September spelling test, A+. Someone had added ten extra plusses, then scrawled *Good job, Smarty Pants* in large, loopy writing. Natalie flipped the page. October spelling test, A+. Here, Annie had crossed out the perfect grade and written, *Oops, I meant F. Love, the Teacher.* Natalie couldn't help smiling.

She skimmed past all her old tests, then came to the note she'd written to herself the day she met Annie.

See how fast you can ride your bike around the block, said the neat cursive words. Natalie sighed. So much had happened since that day, it seemed like years ago. She turned the page, expecting to find a blank sheet. Instead, the rest of the notebook was filled with Annie's huge, wild handwriting. There weren't more than three words per page, she had written so big. The words said:

She left. She left me. I can't believe she left. She left. She left. Why did she leave? She left. The same phrases, over and over until the very last page. She even filled the back cover.

Natalie hugged the notebook to her chest. *Oh Annie,* she thought. *I'm so sorry. I'm sorry your mom left you, I'm sorry I hurt you. I'm sorry for everything.*

Natalie inhaled the earthy smell of the underground room. It reminded her of the first time she came here, when Annie told her the lie about her mom being dead. Those coins she showed Natalie — were they still here? She inched to the spot by the wall where she had watched Annie bury them. Digging into the damp dirt, Natalie felt the chill of metal against her fingertips. She brought the coins into the candlelight and brushed the soil off their faces. Each was stamped with a picture of a circus clown and the words "Resselville Arcade. No cash value."

She turned the coins over and over in her hands. They felt solid and cold against her palms. She felt sad, but not because she found proof that Annie lied. It was because she wished Annie's amazing stories could be real, even though deep down she always knew they weren't. She wanted to believe.

And she wanted to believe that despite everything, there was a way to make things right. She had no idea how to do this, but she suddenly felt a sliver of hope, as thin as the slits of light coming through the floorboards overhead.

Annie said I might be psychic, Natalie thought. *Maybe*

if I sit real still and concentrate, the answer will come to me, just like the boots did.

She folded her fingers around the coins and closed her eyes. She listened to the sound of her own breathing, like the rhythmic rise and fall of waves on the beach, until she heard something else: a tiny voice inside her head. It was quiet, but it was there.

"Ms. Hatch," it said.

"Thank you," Natalie said, pocketing the coins. She spat on the candle and the flame sputtered to smoke.

When Natalie rang Ms. Hatch's doorbell, she realized she had no idea what to say. The psychic voice hadn't gone into detail. *Should I apologize for the secret cards? Or talk about Annie?* Before she could decide, Ms. Hatch opened the door.

"Oh, Natalie!" she said, and shooed Natalie toward a pink poufy chair in the living room. "I knew you'd come. Sit. I'll make some tea."

"How did you know I'd come?" Natalie asked.

"I just had a feeling," the old woman said as she went into the kitchen. She clinked and clanked at the sink for a minute. When she came back into the living room, she was carrying a tray piled with teacups, a teapot, and a plate of sugar cookies. As she placed the tray on the coffee table, she said, "Please do me a favor and eat a lot. I baked too many."

"Thank you," Natalie said meekly. She took a deer-shaped sugar cookie and a napkin. "But please don't be so nice to me. I don't deserve it."

"Oh, hush," Ms. Hatch said. "I bet you think you should apologize for this, don't you?" She picked up a note card from the coffee table, and slipped on the bifocals that hung around her neck. "'Billy Frohman steals Ms. Hatch's pottery and sells each piece for ten dollars,'" she read. "'Her pots and vases are crooked, but people still buy them. She is really a witch, and puts magic potions in all the pots she makes. Watch out, Billy!'"

Natalie cringed. "I'm so sorry."

"Sorry for what? For telling me that people still like my pottery enough to buy it? But that's wonderful news!" she said.

"I mean for calling you a witch," Natalie said. "I don't really think that. Neither does Annie. It was just a joke."

"I have a sense of humor, you know," Ms. Hatch said as she poured the tea. "And what's so bad about being called a witch, anyway? You could've called me a terrible old bore. That would have been much worse."

Natalie shook her head. "Nothing is worse than how everything turned out. The spying was supposed to be just for fun, but I'm afraid we hurt everybody. And I'm afraid there's no way to fix it."

"Oh, people need to lighten up," she said, passing the cream. "What's a little friendly eavesdropping between neighbors? I did it when I was young. And you know what? Most of our neighbors do it, too. They may not hide in lilac bushes or behind a fence, but they peek out their kitchen windows at each other just the same. People are nosy, dear. It's human nature."

Natalie bit the front hooves off her cookie. "It's all such a mess," she said. "With the neighbors. My parents. Annie, too."

"The best thing to do when you're in a mess is to walk right through it. You'll always come out the other side." Ms. Hatch stirred sugar into her tea. "You'll see. Things have a way of working themselves out."

The old woman smiled in an elfish sort of way, her eyes crinkling. It reminded Natalie of the fairy godmother in the red Cinderella storybook she had when she was little. She wished Ms. Hatch could wave a magic wand and make everything right. Abracadabra the neighbors so they were all happy they'd been spied on. Annie would tell Natalie that she didn't hate her anymore. Everyone would say they were brilliant spies and bake them cake. If only.

"Did you know that Annie has been coming to my

house for tea nearly every afternoon since she moved in?" Ms. Hatch asked.

"No," Natalie said. "She never told me."

"We drink tea and eat cookies and she tells me all about her life. She's said so much about your wonderful friendship."

Tears prickled the corners of Natalie's eyes. "We're not friends anymore," she said.

"Though you've had a disagreement with Annie, you still care for her, don't you?"

Natalie nodded.

"No matter how mad you may be with her, you want the best for Annie, right?"

"Yes."

"She thinks of you as her sister, you know."

"Did she really say that?" Natalie asked.

"Yes. Annie doesn't have a family like you have. So she had to make one up. I am like her grand-mother. And you are like her sister."

"My sister." Natalie nodded.

"Well, sisters fight sometimes. But they still love each other. They find a way to be friends again."

"That's true," Natalie said. She felt her sliver of hope expand into a path, wide enough to walk on.

"Before you go, I want to give you a thank-you gift. For discovering that I can still sell my pottery. And for saying I'm a witch."

Ms. Hatch sprang from the couch and went into the other room.

"You've given me the courage to do some witchy things to that Billy Frohman," she called out. "I'm going to set some kind of trap. Maybe I'll grease the top of my fence. Or put superglue on a few of my pots, so Billy's hand gets stuck when he grabs them." She chuckled to herself, then came back into the living room holding a small purple bowl.

"It's beautiful," Natalie said.

"Don't worry," Ms. Hatch said, pressing it into Natalie's hands. "Things will work out."

Chapter Seventeen

From the moment Natalie walked through her front door, she was grounded. Her parents made it clear that she wasn't to leave the house, not even for a bike ride around the block. And no phone calls. No letters. Nothing.

She couldn't go out, but someone came to see her — Mr. Warsaw. He stormed over first thing the next morning. Natalie's dad answered the door while she listened from the top of the stairs.

"I'd like a word with *Olive*," Mr. Warsaw said, his voice quaking.

Natalie's dad called her down. Each stairstep Natalie took, Mr. Warsaw's face grew redder and redder, and his whole body trembled like a teakettle about to whistle. When she reached the bottom step, Mr. Warsaw exploded.

"Who do you think you are, spying on us?" he shouted. "My wife is sick, and mixing her medicine with juice is the only way she'll take it. Don't you know the difference between poison and medicine?"

"I — I'm sorry," Natalie stammered.

"Seeing the pill bottles reminds her that she's sick, and it upsets her, so I have to sort the medicine when she's asleep. You have no idea how much work it is, counting out the pills, and keeping notes about which one Emily needs to take at what time. I'd like to see *you* try it." With that, Mr. Warsaw stomped out the door.

Sergeant Dewey came over too, to say that he was in no way associated with the French government. After thirty years with the U.S. armed forces, the accusation was most insulting. And for her information, making model hot air balloons was a very respectable pastime. Again, Natalie was speechless.

The late-summer air was so hot and stifling that night, Natalie couldn't fall asleep. At close to ten o'clock, she was lying in bed, staring at her new, pink lacy curtains and feeling awful about everything.

There is a difference, she realized, between never having known someone, and knowing a person and then losing her. It's true that both ways you are alone, but they're not the same thing. The first way, you don't miss the person because you never knew her, and you don't even know what to miss. But the second way, you understand how wonderful and special and necessary that person is, so you miss her terribly. *Does Annie still hate me?* Natalie wondered. *Is there any way we can be friends again?*

There was a knock at the bedroom door. Natalie's mom peeked her head in.

"Still awake? There's a call for you," she said, holding out the phone. Natalie sat up in her bed.

"But I'm not allowed phone calls. And it's so late."

"I think it's important," her mom said. Natalie's heart skipped. Was it Annie? She cradled the phone in both hands.

"Hello?" she said.

"Natalie Wallis?" asked an angry voice. It wasn't Annie.

"Yes," Natalie answered.

"This is Trina George."

Oh boy, Natalie thought.

"Thanks to you and your little spying friend," Trina screeched, "I'm grounded from the mall for a month, and I had to give everything back. And just so you know, if you do have photos of us stealing, and you do send them to *Teen Town*, I will personally wreck your life. I have a long career ahead of me as a celebrity and you're not going to ruin my reputation!"

Trina hung up with a slam. Natalie looked over

at her mom, who was standing in the doorway, arms crossed.

"She said — " Natalie began.

"I heard everything from here," her mom said. "She *was* screaming."

"I didn't mean to make anyone feel bad," Natalie said.

"Of course you didn't," her mom scoffed. "But Annie sure did."

Natalie sat up straighter. "We *both* spied. We *both* wrote the note cards."

"Yes, but I'm sure she forced you," her mom said.

"No, she didn't," Natalie said. "You know I'm to blame, too. Why else would I be grounded?"

Her mom sat on the edge of the bed and took a deep breath. "Your dad and I grounded you because we don't want you to see Annie anymore," she said. "She isn't a good friend for you."

"Why?" Natalie asked, her anger rising. "Because she's poor? Or because her uncle works in a bar? Or because she wears weird clothes?"

Surprise mixed with pain on her mom's face. Natalie had never spoken to her like this before. "I didn't say that," her mom said.

"I know Annie's different from me. That's what I like about her."

"You like her *now*," her mom said, twisting a corner of Natalie's blanket. "But what happens in a few years, when she gets into worse things than spying? I just don't want to see my good, smart girl getting into real trouble."

"Mom, Annie's not bad. And I'm not perfect."

Her mom's brow was still furrowed, but her tightly pursed lips began to soften.

"If you really thought I was smart," Natalie continued, "you'd let me decide who's a good friend and who's not. And you'd let me fix my mistakes, not lock me in the house and pretend I had nothing to do with it. Truth is, you don't trust me at all."

Her mom pressed her palms together and touched her fingertips to her mouth, like she was thinking hard. Or praying. She kept her eyes closed for a few moments, and when she opened them again, they were wet.

"I only want the best for you," she said. "But I suppose . . . I suppose I don't always know what that is." She let out a small, sad laugh. "I'm not perfect either, you know."

"Nobody is," Natalie said.

"I'm disappointed that you spied on our neighbors. But you *are* smart. And I *do* trust that you can make things right."

Natalie reached for her mom and pulled her into a tight hug. Her mom stroked her hair, from the roots all the way down to the tips, like she used to do when Natalie was little.

"My precious girl," she said. "Consider yourself officially ungrounded. But now, it's late. Time for bed."

It was past eleven that night. Natalie awoke to a twangy *tap-tap-tap* on the window screen next to her bed. She sat up, squinted away sleep, and brushed her curtains aside. She was startled to see a pair of eyes looking back at her, and a head of short, white-blond hair glowing in the moonlight. Annie.

"Is it really you?" Natalie whispered.

"It's me," Annie said.

Natalie turned her ceiling fan from medium to high to cover the noise, then eased the screen open. She was glad no one had bought the house next door yet — because Annie was hanging in plain view. She crawled inside and landed on the bed with a soft thud.

"Hi."

"Hi."

"I bet you don't want me here," Annie said. Her eyes sparkled like she'd been crying.

"Actually," Natalie said, "I can't think of anyone I'd want to see more."

"I thought you hated me."

"You're the one who said you hated *me*, remember?"

"Oh. Right," Annie said. She looked down at her hands. "I had to come see you. They're talking about moving me to a foster home. It could be miles and miles away."

"Can Ralph really do that? Give you away to a foster home?"

"He can if he wants to." Annie nodded. "Last night, Charla found all her missing cigarettes packs under the couch cushion. She was so mad when she realized she hadn't just lost them, and that I was hiding them, that she told Ralph it was her or me. Guess who he picked." Annie's hands flew up to cover her face. "Nobody wants me," she whispered through tears.

Natalie put her arm around her. "*I* want you," she said. "Annie, you gave me the most fun summer of my whole life. You made me do things I never would've done by myself. And I'm glad. Because I'm not so shy anymore. I'm not afraid of everything anymore. I'm even glad you forced me to talk to Steven, because we're friends now." Natalie put her hand on top of Annie's hand. "If I hadn't met you, I would've spent the whole summer riding my bike around the block."

"You called me a liar," Annie said through sniffles. "What about that?"

"You told some big lies," Natalie admitted. "Why did you say your mom was dead?"

"Ralph and I moved here, and no one knew what had happened. So I made up a story about me and my mom. One that wasn't so sad." Annie let out a quiet sob. "I didn't want to be the girl whose mom left her anymore. Everyone looks at you like you're pathetic. It makes you feel like you'll never be normal again."

"You could've told me the truth. We're friends."

Annie shook her head. "I didn't want you looking at me like that, either."

Natalie nodded. Then she said, "I have something for you." She reached for Ms. Hatch's purple bowl on her nightstand, and poured the two gold tokens it held into Annie's lap.

"My coins," Annie said. She ran her thumb over one of the raised clown faces. "You took them?"

"In case Noah came back to steal more stuff," Natalie said.

"These are from an arcade my mom took me to a little while before she went away," Annie explained. "We stayed there for over three hours playing all the games. These tokens were left over. I kept them because I thought we'd go back sometime." She took a deep, shuddering breath.

"It's not like my mom had anywhere important to go or anyone important to see that day," Annie said. "I guess she just wanted to be anywhere but with me. I had the flu, and she said she'd go buy me some ice cream. She walked out the door and kept on walking. How could she just leave like that? No ice cream. No calls. No letters." Annie stared off into space, in shock, as if she had just gotten the bad news. "She just left. She left. She left," she repeated, dumbstruck.

"Come here," Natalie said. As Annie cried it out, they held hands and watched the ceiling fan spin.

After a long while, Annie said, "The thing is, I really wanted that ice cream. Neapolitan." She let out a combination of a giggle and a sob.

Natalie squeezed her hand. "I'll buy you ice cream. A whole gallon. You can eat it all yourself."

Annie laughed again, which turned into more tears. "I don't want them to send me away," she said.

"I would miss you too much," Natalie said. "And I'd miss your stories, even if they were just lies. That stuff about sign language, was that a lie, too?"

"Yeah."

"Were you actually in a movie?"

"No."

"The freeze pop story?"

"Fake."

"I guess I knew it all along," Natalie said. "I just wished everything was true."

"Thanks, Olive," Annie sniffled. "Truth is, I'm a liar."

"You have a great imagination for stories, that's what. You could be a writer someday."

"You think?"

"Of course you could. I'd buy your book."

"I *am* a little psychic, though," Annie said. "That wasn't a lie. And my powers tell me that you'll do something really great. Like become the president of the United States."

"Ha ha."

"You will. If you're not the president you'll be a spy with the CIA. You have to be a genius to be in the CIA, did you know? You have to pass a million tests."

"Do I get to wear a disguise?"

"You'll have a suitcase full of disguises," Annie said. "They'll ask you to bring your pink cowboy boots along on your secret missions."

✼   ✼   ✼

It was past midnight on Natalie's clock radio. She glanced at Annie, who was breathing the slow, rhythmic breaths of someone who is sleeping. As Natalie looked at her friend, her sister, she felt like maybe if she held her breath and was very still, she could somehow stop time and stay in this moment forever. Make it so that the foster agency never came to take Annie away. Guarantee that the neighbors who were mad at them would always stay asleep.

But Annie finally stirred and sat up.

"I better go. I don't want to fall too deep asleep," she said. "Your parents would find me here in the morning." Annie crawled toward the open window.

"Wait," Natalie said. "I'm coming with you." What if Annie was sent to a new city as soon as tomorrow? Natalie realized this might be her last chance to be with her friend.

Natalie pulled on her pink cowboy boots. Then, carefully, the girls used the drainpipe to crawl down the side of the house. Once their feet touched the grass below, Natalie said, "Let's walk down the alley. For old times' sake."

"Good thinking, Olive," Annie said.

They crossed the street and cut through Annie's yard. The moonlight shone clear and bright on the alley, making it a silvery ribbon between the houses.

"Will you write to me if you leave?" Natalie asked.

"Yeah. I'll even send you a drawing of my new place."

"I'll write to you, too," Natalie said. They walked silently for a few moments before Natalie asked, "How exactly did Charla find the cigarettes?"

"She dropped the TV remote down the crack of the couch, and when she lifted the cushion to get it, she saw all those smashed packs," Annie said. "I told her that cigarettes are unhealthy, and that I was just trying to help her quit. But Ralph took her side, of course. All day, she smoked her flat cigarettes and kept saying, 'You're outta here, kid.'"

Annie imitated Charla's scowl, which made them both giggle.

"Hey," Annie said. "I'm really sorry for telling Steven you like him. For some stupid reason, I thought that was a good idea."

"Don't worry about it," Natalie said. They kept walking, their feet crunching along the sandy alley. Then something caught Annie's attention, and she stopped.

"Olive. Look at that."

Annie pointed to the Warsaws' backyard. There was a figure in a white nightgown drifting slowly across the lawn like a ghost, her arms stretched out at nothing in particular. Her long, white hair hung loose across her shoulders, and though her eyes were open, they weren't focused on anything. It was Mrs. Warsaw. She seemed lost. A twig snapped under Natalie's cowboy boot.

"Grandmother?" Mrs. Warsaw said, her head cocked toward the noise. "Is that you?"

Natalie and Annie looked at each other.

Grandmother? Mrs. Warsaw was at least seventy years old. Her grandmas must be long gone.

What do we do? Natalie mouthed silently.

Help her, Annie mouthed back.

"Mrs. Warsaw?" Annie called out. "Why are you out here?" She walked across the lawn and took the old woman's arm.

"Where is my grandmother?" Mrs. Warsaw asked.

"I'm not sure," Annie replied softly, and motioned for Natalie to follow her. She began leading Mrs. Warsaw toward the back door. "Should we ask your husband?"

"Ask your husband?" Mrs. Warsaw echoed.

Natalie took Mrs. Warsaw's other arm and Annie rang the back doorbell. After a minute, Mr. Warsaw opened the door, wearing blue plaid pajamas and an expression as confused as his wife's.

"Emily?" he said, reaching for Mrs. Warsaw. "What are you doing out here?" He pulled her inside the house, and the girls watched as he sat her on a kitchen chair. "Stay right here," he said. Then he returned to the doorway.

"What were you doing with my wife? And at this hour?" he demanded. "Haven't you snooped on us enough?"

Natalie explained what had happened. Mr. Warsaw's expression became sad.

"She must have wandered out of bed," he said. "My Emily thinks she's a little girl sometimes, and she's forgetful. The medications are supposed to help."

"I have to tell Grandmother," Mrs. Warsaw called out in her urgent, childish tone.

"What does she mean?" Annie asked. "Tell her grandmother what?"

Mr. Warsaw's face tightened again.

"Didn't you hear me? She's confused. She doesn't know what she's talking about," he said.

"We just wanted to help her," Natalie said.

"Then stop prying," he said. He began to close the door, but Annie caught it with her foot.

"Mr. Warsaw," she said, "we're sorry for saying

you were trying to poison your wife. It's obvious you're taking good care of her."

"It's time everyone knew the secret!" Mrs. Warsaw screeched from the kitchen.

"Thank you for your help," he said gruffly. "Good night." He shut the door, and they heard the lock click into place.

"What do you think the secret is?" Annie whispered.

"I don't know," Natalie said. "But we're done spying, remember?"

"Right," Annie said, a smile flickering across her lips. "No more spying."

After deciding there was absolutely no way to shimmy back up the drainpipe to her room, Natalie took a deep breath and rang the front doorbell. Both of her parents answered the door, and both were very unhappy to learn that she had snuck out. For over an hour, they sat in the darkened living room, listening as Natalie explained everything. She told them the truth about Annie's mom, and the possibility that Annie would be sent to a new foster home far away, and how she and Annie had helped a confused Mrs. Warsaw safely back to her house.

When Natalie was done explaining, her parents were still upset about the sneaking out. But as they all climbed the stairs to bed, she felt something had shifted. It was as if her parents began to accept that not everything is perfectly right or wrong, like the number of pills for a prescription or the total on a tax return. Natalie felt as if they started to understand, as she had, that things are usually a bit of both.

Chapter Eighteen

Annie and Natalie were each crouched over a square of sidewalk, busy drawing with chalk. They looked up at each other and smiled. Something wonderful had happened over the last week.

When Ms. Hatch got word that Ralph wanted to send Annie away, she offered to be Annie's new foster parent, or more accurately, foster grandparent. Almost immediately, Annie moved into the guest room on Ms. Hatch's second floor, directly across from Natalie's bedroom window. Ralph and Charla left town as soon as the paperwork was signed and Annie had hauled her last armful of possessions out of the house. Natalie and Annie agreed that when the couple drove off, they probably headed straight to Las Vegas to get married in a drive-through chapel, stopping only for gas and un-smashed cigarettes on the way.

Once Annie was settled into her new house, the girls sat in Ms. Hatch's backyard among the hundreds of pots and vases, and figured out how to set things right with the neighbors. Natalie suggested an apology letter, but they couldn't agree on what to write, so Annie suggested they do an apology drawing instead.

"An apology drawing?" Natalie said. "Does that even exist?"

"Sure. We'll draw a hopscotch board that goes all the way down the block, and back up the other side," Annie explained. "It'll be our present to everyone."

"A present," Natalie said, nodding. It wasn't a bad idea. "I have a full tub of chalk I got for my last birthday. Let's do it."

They began early in the morning in front of Ms. Hatch's house on the corner, with the "one" square and big block letters that said, "Start Here." They added square after square until they reached Virginia Brooks's sidewalk, and there, instead of continuing to draw plain hopscotch boxes, they started adding different shapes like circles, hearts, and stars. And instead of continuing to fill the shapes with numbers, they wrote words. They wrote all the words that reminded them of their summer together. Freeze pop. Whisper. Cowboy boots. Sister. When they ran out of favorite words, they switched to directions, like "Dance to the end of this square" and "Write down your favorite animal (chalk is to your left)."

By late afternoon, they were stationed in front of Steven Redding's house, colorful chalk sticks strewn around them like spilled donut sprinkles. Annie was drawing the cloud town she never had a chance to finish on her bedroom wall at Ralph's. There were cloud people living in cloud palaces, eating cloud suppers, and listening to cloud music. For hopscotchers to pass Annie's cloud square, they'd have to tiptoe between the palaces without touching any lines. Meanwhile, Natalie sketched an enormous horse two sidewalk squares long. Steven watched over her shoulder as she drew the big, rectangular teeth.

"See, when you get to this part, you have to toss the rock so it lands right in the horse's mouth, like a sugar cube. Then you have to jump with both feet on the horse's back, pick up the rock, and then you can pass to the next square."

"That's so creative," Steven said.

Natalie blushed, and held up a piece of chalk to him. "Want to help?" she asked.

"We need it," Annie added, looking down the block at the bare sidewalk. "There are six houses to go."

"Nah," Steven said. "I'm no good at drawing. But I do want a turn on the board when you're done. So, I'll see you later?"

"See you," Natalie said, waving as he turned to go.

Once Steven was inside his house, Annie whispered, "He totally likes you."

"He just wants to be friends," Natalie said. But secretly, she wished Annie was right. Maybe he did like her, just a teeny tiny bit?

As the girls drew, they occasionally saw curious faces peering out of windows and screen doors. A few people waved and smiled, including Mrs. Warsaw. Mrs. Turner actually came out to visit them, and said she was glad the girls had spied on her, because it gave her the courage to tell her husband that she wanted to travel. Now, he was helping her plan a January trip to Brazil. With great excitement, Mrs. Turner showed them the envelope that held her plane tickets.

After Mrs. Turner had gone, Annie said, "Hey, did you notice how Noah only gave people secret cards about themselves?"

"That's true," Natalie said. "Why didn't he give everyone someone else's secret? That would've been way worse."

"Because, Olive, he's dumb. I don't think it ever

crossed his mind." She colored in the outline of a cloud with light blue.

"Noah," Natalie sighed. "I wish we could get back at him somehow."

"Don't worry. I took care of him the first day you were grounded," Annie said. "I told him if he messes with us again, I'll make sure everyone finds out his big secret."

"What's his big secret?" Natalie asked.

"Who knows?" Annie shrugged. "I never spied on him. But he must have a pretty big one, because he was scared."

"You're a genius, Elvis."

"Why thank you, Olive. There's just one problem. I think he likes me now. He found out that I like dead birds and stuff, and I'm his new hero." Annie rolled her eyes. "He actually brought me a dead mouse yesterday. Like a cat does."

"Maybe you'll marry Noah, and I'll marry Steven, and then we can really be sisters," Natalie teased.

"Ha ha."

"Too bad everyone knows our code names now," Natalie said. "Elvis and Olive aren't secret anymore."

"So what?" Annie said. "We can still use them. I'm Elvis no matter what. And you're Olive no matter what."

Just then, there was the sound of Albert Castle's car door slamming. He stepped out onto the curb in his business suit and, clenching his briefcase, he stared down at the girls' drawing for a full minute. Then, long arms swinging, he walked to the corner, where Annie had written "Start Here." Albert strolled the length of the hopscotch board slowly, as if completing each move in his mind. Natalie and Annie just watched him. When he reached the opposite corner, he hopped the world's smallest hop — just a centimeter off the ground. Then he turned to the girls and gave them a graceful nod, almost like a bow.

"See?" Annie whispered. "Our plan is working."

Natalie savored Albert's forgiving nod. But even more meaningful was when her mom came outside with lemonade and brownies. She offered the treats to both Natalie and Annie, and while they ate, she admired their work. She said she especially loved Annie's cloud town — it reminded her of a drawing she made when she was a girl. Before she went back inside, Natalie's mom touched each girl on the head and smiled.

Though Natalie's drawing hand was sore, and she was hot and tired, her mom's kind gesture kept her going all the way down to the corner, to the very last square. There, she and Annie simply signed their not-so-secret code names in big, bright letters.

"Hey," Natalie said, setting down her chalk. "Want to know the sign for something that turns out well, even though it was a big mess?" Annie finished writing the S in *Elvis* and looked up.

"So you know sign language now?" she asked cautiously.

"Yep. Learned it from a friend. You kind of make it up as you go, from what I can tell."

"I see," Annie said. "So what's the sign?"

Natalie made a sad face and wiggled her fingers in a tangled bunch. Then she turned her palms up to the sky, as if she was going to catch something precious, and smiled. Annie repeated the sign back to her.

"I'll miss you in September," Natalie said. "I wish you went to my school."

Annie gave her shoulder a nudge. "You're acting like we won't live across the street from each other. I'll see you practically every day."

"You swear?" Natalie asked.

Annie clapped a chalk-dusted hand over her heart. "I swear on our dead bird and my mom's imaginary grave."

In the four days the record-length hopscotch board lasted, before the big rainstorm, it became rather famous. Kids from as far as six blocks away came to take a turn. Some people even took pictures. And every day, more and more of Natalie's neighbors came out of their houses to have a closer look. Every time she saw someone smiling down at the drawing, she felt forgiven.

Of course, some people weren't so generous. Trina George, for one. She sneered at Natalie from her lounge chair whenever Natalie passed on her bike, but Natalie actually saw this as an improvement: At least Trina was acknowledging her existence now. Virginia Brooks would gasp and run the other way whenever she saw Natalie or Annie. Natalie just hoped they hadn't driven Ms. Brooks to eat more than her usual amount of face cream.

The night before school started, as Natalie was putting on her pajamas, she felt a pang of loneliness. The summer was officially over. Once again, her life would be filled with schedules and teachers and homework. She'd see her old friends, who were nice girls, but weren't Annie. She couldn't wear her pink cowboy boots all day anymore — they weren't part of the official school uniform.

But Natalie also felt a twinge of excitement, because the backpack her mom bought her smelled new and was full of fresh notebooks. Steven knew her name. She was starting fifth grade. And Annie lived right across the street now, with Natalie's bedroom facing hers so they could wish each other good night with flashlights.

After Natalie brushed her teeth, she waited by her darkened bedroom window, her pink flashlight ready on the sill. Soon, an orb of light appeared in the upstairs of Ms. Hatch's house. Annie pointed her flashlight down at the street, and Natalie touched the pale ray with her own. They chased each other's lights across the neighbors' lawns and flower beds, up walls and onto roofs, and to the stop sign and back. Then Annie aimed her beam straight at Natalie's window and performed her half of the official signal: *On-off-onnnnnnnn-off*. That meant "good."

Natalie sent the reply right back: *On-off-onoffonoff-onnnnnnnn*. During the last *on*, she traced a wide circle in the sky. That meant "night."

Thank-Yous

To those who helped welcome this book into the world,
I owe my deepest thanks:

Ali Hensinger, Julia Kenny, Jacque Fletcher, Katy Holmgren,
Cathy Clark, Mélina Mangal, Jayne Ubl, and Gretchen
Brandt — the brave souls who critiqued my early drafts

Karen and Steve Watson, for the unwavering support
of my artistic shenanigans

Lisa Watson, switchboard operator of the
Encouragement and Advice Hotline

Marcelo Ferraz de Toledo — my rock

Joy Tutela, for guidance and enthusiasm from the start

And Kara LaReau, editor of my dreams and patron saint
of Elvis and Olive

About the Author

Stephanie Watson lives and works in St. Paul, Minnesota. *Elvis & Olive* is her first book for young readers. She says, "I really wanted to write a children's book, and I wasn't sure I could do it, so for a long time I kept the writing of this story a secret. And before I knew it, the story was about secrets." You can learn more about Stephanie at her website, www.stephanie-watson.com